To Winifred
From Mother
1931

TED WADED OUT, AND BROUGHT HIS SISTER'S DOLL TO SHORE.

The Curlytops on Star Island Page 18

THE CURLYTOPS
ON
STAR ISLAND

OR

Camping out with Grandpa

BY

HOWARD R. GARIS

AUTHOR OF "THE CURLYTOPS SERIES," "BEDTIME
STORIES," "UNCLE WIGGILY SERIES," ETC.

Illustrations by
JULIA GREENE

NEW YORK
CUPPLES & LEON COMPANY

THE CURLYTOPS SERIES

By HOWARD R. GARIS

12mo. Cloth. Illustrated.

THE CURLYTOPS AT CHERRY FARM
   Or, Vacation Days in the Country
THE CURLYTOPS ON STAR ISLAND
   Or, Camping Out With Grandpa
THE CURLYTOPS SNOWED IN
   Or, Grand Fun With Skates and Sleds
THE CURLYTOPS AT UNCLE FRANK'S RANCH
   Or, Little Folks on Ponyback

CUPPLES & LEON COMPANY, New York

Copyright, 1918, by
Cupples & Leon Company

The Curlytops on Star Island
Printed in U. S. A.

CONTENTS

CHAPTER		PAGE
I	THE BLUE LIGHT	1
II	WHAT THE FARMER TOLD	14
III	OFF TO STAR ISLAND	32
IV	OVERBOARD	42
V	THE BAG OF SALT	56
VI	TED AND THE BEAR	67
VII	JAN SEES SOMETHING	78
VIII	TROUBLE FALLS IN	91
IX	TED FINDS A CAVE	101
X	THE GRAPEVINE SWING	111
XI	TROUBLE MAKES A CAKE	123
XII	THE CURLYTOPS GO SWIMMING	139
XIII	JAN'S QUEER RIDE	157
XIV	DIGGING FOR GOLD	164

Contents

CHAPTER		PAGE
XV	THE BIG HOLE	175
XVI	A GLAD SURPRISE	188
XVII	TROUBLE'S PLAYHOUSE	197
XVIII	IN THE CAVE	211
XIX	THE BLUE LIGHT AGAIN	224
XX	THE HAPPY TRAMP	236

THE CURLYTOPS
ON
STAR ISLAND

CHAPTER I

THE BLUE LIGHT

"MOTHER, make Ted stop!"

"I'm not doing anything at all, Mother!"

"Yes he is, too! Please call him in. He's hurting my doll."

"Oh, Janet Martin, I am not!"

"You are so, Theodore Baradale Martin; and you've just got to stop!"

Janet, or Jan, as she was more often called, stood in front of her brother with flashing eyes and red cheeks.

"Children! Children! What are you doing now?" asked their mother, appearing in the doorway of the big, white farmhouse, holding in her arms a small boy. "Please don't make so much noise. I've just gotten Baby William to sleep, and if he wakes up——"

"Yes, don't wake up Trouble, Jan," added Theodore, or Ted, the shorter name being the one by which he was most often called. "If you do he'll want to come with us, and we can't make Nicknack race."

"I wasn't waking him up, it was you!" exclaimed Jan. "He keeps pulling my doll's legs, Mother and——"

"I only pulled 'em a little bit, just to see if they had any springs in 'em. Jan said her doll was a circus lady and could jump on the back of a horse. I wanted to see if she had any springs in her legs."

"Well, I'm *pretending* she has, so there, Ted Martin! And if you don't stop——"

"There now, please stop, both of you, and be nice," begged Mrs. Martin. "I thought, since you had your goat and wagon, you could play without having so much fuss. But, if you can't——"

"Oh, we'll be good!" exclaimed Ted, running his hands through his tightly curling hair, but not taking any of the kinks out that way. "We'll be good. I won't tease Jan any more."

"You'd better not!" warned his sister, and, though she was a year younger than Ted, she did not seem at all afraid of him.

The Blue Light

"If you do I'll take my half of the goat away and you can't ride."

"Pooh! Which is your half?" asked Ted.

"The wagon. And if you don't have the wagon to hitch Nicknack to, how're you going to ride?"

"Huh! I could ride on his back. Take your old wagon if you want to, but if you do——"

"The-o-dore!" exclaimed his mother in a slow, warning voice, and when he heard his name spoken in that way, with each syllable pronounced separately, Ted knew it was time to haul down his quarreling colors and behave. He did it this time.

"I—I'm sorry," he faltered. "I didn't mean that, Jan. I won't pull your doll's legs any more."

"And I won't take the goat-wagon away. We'll both go for a ride in it."

"That's the way to have a good time," said Mrs. Martin, with a smile. "Now don't make any more noise, for William is fussy. Run off and play now, but don't go too far."

"We'll go for a ride," said Teddy. "Come on, Jan. You can let your doll make-believe drive the goat if you want to."

"Thank you, Teddy. But I guess I'd better not. I'll pretend she's a Red Cross nurse and I'm taking her to the hospital to work."

"Then we'll make-believe the goat-wagon is an ambulance!" exclaimed Ted. "And I'm the driver and I don't mind the big guns. Come on, that'll be fun!"

Filled with the new idea, the two children hurried around the side of the farmhouse out toward the barn where Nicknack, their pet goat, was kept. Mrs. Martin smiled as she saw them go.

"Well, there'll be quiet for a little while," she said, "and William can have his sleep."

"What's the matter, Ruth?" asked an old gentleman coming up the walk just then. "Have the Curlytops been getting into mischief again?"

"No. Teddy and Janet were just having one of their little quarrels. It's all over now. You look tired, Father."

Grandpa Martin was Mrs. Martin's husband's father, but she loved him as though he were her own.

"Yes, I am tired. I've been working pretty hard on the farm," said Grandpa Martin, "but I'm going to rest a bit now. Want me to take Trouble?" he asked as he saw the little boy in his mother's arms. Baby

The Blue Light

William was called Trouble because he got into so much of it.

"No, thank you. He's asleep," said Mother Martin. "But I do wish you could find some way to keep Ted and Jan from disputing and quarreling so much."

"Oh, they don't act half as bad as lots of children."

"No, indeed! They're very good, I think," said Grandma Martin, coming to the door with a patch of flour on the end of her nose, for it was baking day, as you could easily have told had you come anywhere near the big kitchen of the white house on Cherry Farm.

"They need to be kept busy all the while," said Grandpa Martin. "It's been a little slow for them here this vacation since we got in the hay and gathered the cherries. I think I'll have to find some new way for them to have fun."

"I didn't know there was any new way," said Mother Martin with a laugh, as she carried Baby William into the bedroom and came back to sit on the porch with Grandpa and Grandma Martin.

"Oh, yes, there are lots of new ways. I haven't begun to think of them yet," said

Grandpa Martin. "I'm going to have a few weeks now with not very much to do until it's time to gather the fall crops, and I think I'll try to find some way of giving your Curlytops a good time. Yes, that's what I'll do. I'll keep the Curlytops so busy they won't have a chance to think of pulling dolls' legs or taking Nicknack, the goat, away from his wagon."

"What are you planning to do, Father?" asked Grandma Martin of her husband.

"Well, I promised to take them camping on Star Island you know."

"What! Not those two little tots—not Ted and Jan?" cried Grandma Martin, looking up in surprise.

"Yes, indeed, those same Curlytops!"

It was easy to understand why Grandpa Martin, as well as nearly everyone else, called the two Martin children Curlytops. It was because their hair was so tightly curling to their heads. Once Grandma Martin lost her thimble in the hair of one of the children, and their locks were curled so nearly alike that she never could remember on whose head she found the needle-pusher.

"Do you think it will be safe to take Ted and Jan camping?" asked Mother Martin.

"Why, yes. There's no finer place in the country than Star Island. And if you go along——"

"Am I to go?" asked Ted's mother.

"Of course. And Trouble, too. It'll do you all good. I wish Dick could come, too," went on Grandpa Martin, speaking of Ted's father, who had gone from Cherry Farm for a few days to attend to some matters at a store he owned in the town of Cresco. "But Dick says he'll be too busy. So I guess the Curlytops will have to go camping with grandpa," added the farmer, smiling.

"Well, I'm sure they couldn't have better fun than to go with you," replied Mother Martin. "But I'm not sure that Baby William and I can go."

"Oh, yes you can," said her father-in-law. "We'll talk about it again. But here come Ted and Jan now in the goat-cart. They seem to have something to ask you. We'll talk about the camp later."

Teddy and Janet Martin, the two Curlytops, came riding up to the farmhouse in a small wagon drawn by a fine, big goat, that they had named Nicknack.

"Please, Mother," begged Ted, "may we ride over to the Home and get Hal?"

"We promised to take him for a ride," added Jan.

"Yes, I suppose you may go," said Mother Martin. "But you must be careful, and be home in time for supper."

"We will," promised Ted. "We'll go by the wood-road, and then we won't get run over by any automobiles. They don't come on that road."

"All right. Now remember—don't stay too late."

"No, we won't!" chorused the two children, and down the garden path and along the lane they went to a road that led through Grandpa Martin's wood-lot and so on to the Home for Crippled Children, which was about a mile from Cherry Farm.

Among others at the Home was a lame boy named Hal Chester. That is, he had been lame when the Curlytops first met him early in the summer, but he was almost cured now, and walked with only a little limp. The Home had been built to cure lame children, and had helped many of them.

Half-way to the big red building, which was like a hospital, the Curlytops met Hal, the very boy whom they had started out to see.

"Hello, Hal!" cried Ted. "Get in and have a ride."

"Thanks, I will. I was just coming over to see you, anyway. What are you two going to do?"

"Nothing much," Ted answered, while Jan moved along the seat with her doll, to make room for Hal. "What're you going to do?"

"Same as you."

The three children laughed at that.

"Let's ride along the river road," suggested Janet. "It'll be nice and shady there, and if my Red Cross doll is going to the war she'll like to be cool once in a while."

"Is your doll a Red Cross nurse?" asked Hal. "If she is, where's her cap and the red cross on her arm?"

"Oh, she just started to be a nurse a little while ago," Jan explained. "I haven't had time to make the red cross yet. But I will. Anyhow, let's go down by the river."

"All right, we will," agreed Ted. "We'll see if we can get some sticks off the willow trees and make whistles," he added to Hal.

"You can make better whistles in the spring, when the bark is softer, than you can now," said the lame boy, as the Curlytops often called him, though Hal was nearly cured.

"Well, *maybe* we can make some now," suggested Ted, and a little later the two boys were seated in the shade under the willow trees that grew on the bank of a small river which flowed into Clover Lake, not far from Cherry Farm. Nicknack, tied to a tree, nibbled the sweet, green grass, and Jan made a wreath of buttercups for her doll.

After they had made some whistles, which did give out a little tooting sound, Ted and Hal found something else to do, and Jan saw, coming along the road, a girl named Mary Seaton with whom she often played. Jan called Mary to join her, and the two little girls had a good time together while Ted and Hal threw stones at some wooden boats they made and floated down the stream.

"Oh, Ted, we must go home!" suddenly cried Jan. "It's getting dark!"

The sun was beginning to set, but it would not really have been dark for some time, except that the western sky was filled with clouds that seemed to tell of a coming storm. So, really, it did appear as though night were at hand.

The Blue Light 11

"I guess we'd better go," Ted said, with a look at the dark clouds. "Come on, Hal. There's room for you, too, Mary, in the wagon."

"Can Nicknack pull us all?" Mary asked.

"I guess so. It's mostly down hill. Come on!"

The four children got into the goat-wagon, and if Nicknack minded the bigger load he did not show it, but trotted off rather fast. Perhaps he knew he was going home to his stable where he would have some sweet hay and oats to eat, and that was what made him so glad to hurry along.

The wagon was stopped near the Home long enough to let Hal get out, and a little later Mary was driven up to her gate. Then Ted and Jan, with the doll between them, drove on.

"Oh, Ted!" exclaimed his sister, "mother'll scold. We oughtn't to have stayed so late. It's past supper time!"

"We didn't mean to. Anyhow, I guess they'll give us something to eat. Grandma baked cookies to-day and there'll be some left."

"I hope so," replied Jan with a sigh. "I'm hungry!"

They drove on in silence a little farther, and then, as they came to the top of a hill and could look down toward Star Island in the middle of Clover Lake, Ted suddenly called:

"Look, Jan!"

"Where?" she asked.

"Over there," and her brother pointed to the island. "Do you see that blue light?"

"On the island, do you mean? Yes, I see it. Maybe somebody's there with a lantern."

"Nobody lives on Star Island. Besides, who'd have a blue lantern?"

Jan did not answer.

It was now quite dark, and down in the lake, where there was a patch of black which was Star Island, could be seen a flickering blue glow, that seemed to stand still and then move about.

"Maybe it's lightning bugs," suggested Jan.

"Huh! Fireflies are sort of white," exclaimed Ted. "I never saw a light like that before."

"Me, either, Ted! Hurry up home. Giddap, Nicknack!" and Jan threw at the goat a pine cone, one of several she had picked up and put in the wagon when they were taking a rest in the woods that afternoon.

Nicknack gave a funny little wiggle to his tail, which the children could hardly see in the darkness, and then he trotted on faster. The Curlytops, looking back, had a last glimpse of the flickering blue light as they hurried toward Cherry Farm, and they were a little frightened.

"What do you s'pose it is?" asked Jan.

"I don't know," answered Ted. "We'll ask Grandpa. Go on, Nicknack!"

CHAPTER II

WHAT THE FARMER TOLD

"WELL, where in the world have you children been?"

"Didn't you know we'd be worried about you?"

"Did you get lost again?"

Mother Martin, Grandpa Martin and Grandma Martin took turns asking these three questions as Ted and Jan drove up to the farmhouse in the darkness a little later.

"You said you wouldn't stay late," went on Mother Martin, as the Curlytops got out of the goat-wagon.

"We didn't mean to, Mother," said Ted.

"Oh, but we're so scared!" exclaimed Jan, and as Grandma Martin put her arms about the little girl she felt Jan's heart beating faster than usual.

"Why, what is the matter?" asked the old lady.

What the Farmer Told 15

"Me wants a wide wif Nicknack!" demanded Baby William, as he stood beside his mother in the doorway.

"No, Trouble. Not now," answered Ted. "Nicknack is tired and has to have his supper. Is there any supper left for us?" he asked eagerly.

"Well, I guess we can find a cold potato, or something like it, for such tramps as you," laughed Grandpa Martin. "But where on earth have you been, and what kept you?"

Then Ted put Nicknack in the barn. But when he came back he and Jan between them told of having stayed playing later than they meant to.

"Well, you got home only just in time," said Mother Martin as she took the children to the dining-room for a late supper. "It's starting to rain now."

And so it was, the big drops pelting down and splashing on the windows.

"But what frightened you, Jan?" asked Grandma Martin.

"It was a queer blue light on Star Island."

"A light on Star Island!" exclaimed her grandfather. "Nonsense! Nobody stays on the island after dark unless it's a fisherman or two, and the fish aren't biting well enough now to make anyone stay late to try to catch them. You must have dreamed it—or made-believe."

"No, we really saw it!" declared Ted. "It was a fliskering blue light."

"Well, if there's any such thing there as a 'fliskering' blue light we'll soon find out what it is," said Grandpa Martin.

"How?" asked Ted, his eyes wide open in wonder.

"By going there to see what it is. I'm going to take you two Curlytops to camp on Star Island, and if there's anything queer there we'll see what it is."

"Oh, are we really going to live on Star Island?" gasped Janet.

"Camping out with grandpa! Oh, what fun!" cried Ted. "Do you mean it?" and he looked anxiously at the farmer, fearing there might be some joke about it.

"Oh, I really mean it," said Grandpa Martin. "Though I hardly believe you saw a real light on the island. It must have been a firefly."

"Lightning bugs aren't that color," declared Ted. "It was a blue light, almost like

What the Farmer Told

Fourth of July. But tell us about camping, Grandpa!"

"Yes, please do," begged Jan.

And while the children are eating their late supper, and Grandpa Martin is telling them his plans, I will stop just a little while to make my new readers better acquainted with the Curlytops and their friends.

You have already met Theodore, or Teddy or Ted, Martin, and his sister Janet, or Jan. With their mother, they were spending the long summer vacation on Cherry Farm, the country home of Grandpa Martin outside the town of Elmburg, near Clover Lake. Mr. Richard Martin, or Dick, as Grandpa Martin called him, owned a store in Cresco, where he lived with his family. Besides Ted and Jan there was Baby William, aged about three years. He was called Trouble, for the reason I have told you, though Mother Martin called him "Dear Trouble" to make up for the fun Ted and Jan sometimes poked at him.

Then there was Nora Jones, the maid who helped Mrs. Martin with the cooking and housework. And I must not forget Skyrocket, a dog, nor Turnover, a cat. These did not help with the housework—though I suppose you might say they did, too, in a way, for they ate the scraps from the table and this helped to save work.

In the first book of this series, called "The Curlytops at Cherry Farm," I had the pleasure of telling you how Jan and Ted, with their father, mother and Nora went to grandpa's place in the country to spend the happy vacation days. On the farm, which was named after the number of cherry trees on it, the Curlytops found a stray goat which they were allowed to keep, and they got a wagon which Nicknack (the name they gave their new pet) drew with them in it.

Having the goat made up for having to leave the dog and the cat at home, and Nicknack made lots of good times for Ted and Jan. In the book you may read of the worry the children carried because Grandpa Martin had lost money on account of a flood at his farm, and so could not help when there was a fair and collection for the Crippled Children's Home.

But, most unexpectedly, the cherries helped when Mr. Sam Sander, the lollypop man, bought them from Grandpa Martin, and found a way of making them into candy. And when Ted and Jan and Trouble

What the Farmer Told

were lost in the woods once, the lollypop man——

But I think you would rather read the story for yourself in the other book. I will just say that the Curlytops were still at Cherry Farm, though Father Martin had gone away for a little while. And now, having told you about the family, I'll go back where I left off, and we'll see what is happening.

"Yes," said Grandpa Martin, "I think I will take you Curlytops to camp on Star Island. Camping will do you good. You'll learn lots in the woods there. And won't it be fun to live in a tent?"

"Oh, won't it though!" cried Ted, and the shine in Jan's eyes and the glow on her red cheeks showed how happy she was.

"But I'd like to know what that blue light was," said the little girl.

"Oh, don't worry about that!" laughed Grandpa Martin. "I'll get that blue light and hang it in our tent for a lantern."

I think I mentioned that Jan and Ted had such wonderful curling hair that even strangers, seeing them the first time, called them the "Curlytops." And Ted, who was aged seven years, with his sister just a year younger (their anniversaries coming on exactly the same day) did not in the least mind being called this. He and Jan rather liked it.

"Let's don't go to bed yet," said Jan to her brother, as they finished supper and went from the dining-room into the sitting-room, where they were allowed to play and have good times if they did not get too rough. And they did not often do this.

"All right. It *is* early," Ted agreed. "But what can we do?"

"Let's pretend we have a camp here," went on Jan.

"Where?" asked Ted.

"Right in the sitting-room," answered Jan. "We can make-believe the couch is a tent, and we can crawl under it and go to sleep."

"I wants to go to sleeps there!" cried Trouble. "I wants to go to sleeps right now!"

"Shall we take him back to mother?" asked Ted, looking at his sister. "If he's sleepy now he won't want to play."

"I isn't too sleepy to play," objected Baby William. "I can go to sleeps under couch if you wants me to," he added.

What the Farmer Told

"Oh, that'll be real cute!" cried Janet. "Come on, Ted, let's do it! We can make-believe Trouble is our little dog, or something like that, to watch over our tent, and he can go to sleep——"

"Huh! how's he going to *watch* if he goes to *sleep?*" Ted demanded.

"Oh, well, he can make-believe go to sleep or make-believe watch, either one," explained Janet.

"Yes, I s'pose he could do that," agreed Teddy.

Baby William opened his mouth wide and yawned.

"I guess he'll do some *real* sleeping," said Janet with a laugh. "Come on, Trouble, before you get your eyes so tight shut you can't open 'em again. Come on, we'll play camping!" and she led the way into the sitting room and over toward the big couch at one end.

Many a good time the children had had in this room, and the old couch, pretty well battered and broken now, had been in turn a fort, a steamboat, railroad car, and an automobile. That was according to the particular make-believe game the children were playing. Now the old couch was to be a tent, and Jan and Ted moved some chairs, which would be part of the pretend-camp, up in front of it.

"It'll be a lot of fun when we go camping for real," said Teddy, as he helped his sister spread one of Grandma Martin's old shawls over the backs of some chairs. This was to be a sort of second tent where they could make-believe cook their meals.

"Yes, we'll have grand fun," agreed Jan. "No, you mustn't go to sleep up there, Trouble!" she called to the little fellow, for he had crawled up on top of the couch and had stretched himself out as though to take a nap.

"Why?" he asked.

" 'Cause the tent part is under it," explained his sister. "That's the top of the tent where you are. You can't go to sleep on *top* of a tent. You might fall off."

"I can fall off now!" announced Trouble, as he suddenly thought of something. Then he gave a wiggle and rolled off the seat, bumping into Ted, who had stooped down to put a rug under the couch-tent.

"Ouch!" cried Ted. "Look out what you're doing, Trouble! You bumped my head."

"I—I bumped *my* head!" exclaimed the little fellow, rubbing his tangled hair.

"He didn't mean to," said Janet. "You mustn't roll off that way, Trouble. You might be hurt. Come now, go to sleep under the couch. That's inside the tent you know."

She showed him where Ted had spread the rug, as far back under the couch as he could reach, and this looked to Trouble like a nice place.

"I go to sleeps in there!" he said, and under the couch he crawled, growling and grunting.

"What are you doing that for?" asked Ted, in some surprise.

"I's a bear!" exclaimed Baby William. "I's a bad bear! Burr-r-r-r!" and he growled again.

"Oh, you mustn't do that!" objected Janet. "We don't want any bears in our camp!"

"Course we can have 'em!" cried Ted. "That'll be fun! We'll play Trouble is a bear 'stead of a dog, and I can hunt him. Only I ought to have something for a gun. I know! I'll get grandpa's Sunday cane!" and he started for the hall.

"Oh, no. I don't want to play bear and hunting!" objected Janet.

"Why not?"

" 'Cause it's too—too—scary at night. Let's play something nice and quiet. Let Trouble be our watch dog, and we can be in camp and he can bark and scare something."

"What'll he scare?" asked Ted.

Meanwhile Baby William was crawling as far back under the couch as he could, growling away, though whether he was pretending to be a bear, a lion or only a dog no one knew but himself.

"What do you want him to scare?" asked Ted of his sister.

"Oh—oh—well, chickens, maybe!" she answered.

"Pooh! Chickens aren't any fun!" cried Ted. "If Trouble is going to be a dog let him scare a wild bull, or something like that. Anyhow chickens don't come to camp."

"Well, neither does wild bulls!" declared Janet.

"Yes, they do!" cried Ted, and it seemed as if there would be so much talk that the children would never get to playing anything. "Don't you 'member how daddy told us about going camping, and in the night a wild bull almost knocked down the tent."

"Well, that was real, but this is only make-believe," said Janet. "Let Trouble scare the chickens."

"All right," agreed Ted, who was nearly always kind to his sister. "Go on and growl, Trouble. You're a dog and you're going to scare the chickens out of camp."

They waited a minute but Trouble did not growl.

"Why don't you make a noise?" asked Janet.

Trouble gave a grunt.

"What's the matter?" asked Ted.

"I—I can't growl 'cause I'm all stuck under here," answered the voice of the little fellow, from far under the couch. "I can't wiggle!"

"Oh, dear!" cried Janet.

Teddy stooped and looked beneath the couch.

"He's caught on some of the springs that stick down," he said. "I'll poke him out."

He caught hold of Trouble's clothes and pulled the little fellow loose. But Trouble cried—perhaps because he was sleepy—and then his mother came and got him, leaving

Teddy and Janet to play by themselves, which they did until they, too, began to feel sleepy.

"You'll want to go to bed earlier than this when you go camping, my Curlytops," said Grandpa Martin, as the children came out of the sitting-room.

"Are you really going to take them camping?" asked Mother Martin after Jan and Ted had gone upstairs to bed.

"I really am. There are some tents in the barn. I own part of Star Island and there's no nicer place to camp. You'll come, too, and so will Dick when he comes back from Cresco. We'll take Nora along to do the cooking. Will you come, Mother?" and the Curlytops' grandfather looked at his gray-haired wife.

"No, I'll stay on Cherry Farm and feed the hired men," she answered with a smile.

"Why do they call it Star Island?" asked Ted's mother.

"Well, once upon a time, a good many years ago," said Grandpa Martin, "a shooting star, or meteor, fell blazing on the island, and that's how it got its name."

"Maybe it was a part of the star shining that the children saw to-night," said Grand-

What the Farmer Told

ma Martin. "Though I don't see how it could be, for it fell many years ago."

"Maybe," agreed her husband.

None of them knew what a queer part that fallen star was to have in the lives of those who were shortly to go camping on the island.

Early the next morning after breakfast, Ted and Jan went out to the barn to get Nicknack to have a ride.

"Where is you? I wants to come, too!" cried the voice of their little brother, as they were putting the harness on their goat.

"Oh, there's Trouble," whispered Ted. "Shall we take him with us, Jan?"

"Yes, this time. We're not going far. Grandma wants us to go to the store for some baking soda."

"All right, we'll drive down," returned Ted. "Come on, Trouble!" he called.

"I's tummin'," answered Baby William. "I's dot a tookie."

"He means cookie," said Jan, laughing.

"I know it," agreed Ted. "I wish he'd bring me one."

"Me too!" exclaimed Janet.

"I's dot a 'ot of tookies," went on Trouble, who did not always talk in such "baby fashion." When he tried to he could speak very well, but he did not often try.

"Oh, he's got his whole apron *full* of cookies!" cried Jan. "Where did you get them?" she asked, as her little brother came into the barn.

"Drandma given 'em to me, an' she said you was to have some," announced the little boy, as he let the cookies slide out of his apron to a box that stood near the goat-wagon.

Then Baby William began eating a cookie, and Jan and Ted did also, for they, too, were hungry, though it was not long after breakfast.

"Goin' to wide?" asked Trouble, his mouth full of cookie.

"Yes, we're going for a ride," answered Jan. "Oh, Ted, get a blanket or something to put over our laps. It's awful dusty on the road to-day, even if it did rain last night. It all dried up, I guess."

"All right, I'll get a blanket from grandpa's carriage. And you'd better get a cushion for Trouble."

"I will," said Janet, and her brother and sister left Baby William alone with the goat for a minute or two.

When Jan came back with the cushion she went to get another cookie, but there were none.

"Why Trouble Martin!" she cried, "did you eat them *all?*"

"All what?"

"All the cookies!"

"I did eat one and Nicknack—he did eat the west. He was hungry, he was, and he did eat the west ob 'em. I feeded 'em to him. Nicknack was a hungry goat," said Trouble, smiling.

"I should think he was hungry, to eat up all those cookies! I only had one!" cried Jan.

"What! Did Nicknack get at the cookies?" cried Ted, coming back with a light lap robe.

"Trouble gave them to him," explained Janet. "Oh dear! I was so hungry for another!"

"I'll ask grandma for some," promised Ted, and he soon came back with his hands full of the round, brown molasses cookies.

"Hello, Curlytops, what can I do for you to-day?" asked the storekeeper a little later, when the three children had driven up to his front door. "Do you want a barrel of sugar put in your wagon or a keg of salt mack'rel? I have both."

"We want baking soda," answered Jan.

"And you shall have the best I've got. Where are you going—off to look for the end of the rainbow and get the pot of gold at the end?" he asked jokingly.

"No, we're not going far to-day," answered Ted.

"Well, stop in when you're passing this way again," called out the storekeeper as Ted turned Nicknack around for the homeward trip. "I'm always glad to see you."

"Maybe you won't see us now for quite a while," answered Jan proudly.

"No? Why not? You're not going to leave Cherry Farm I hope."

Ted stopped Nicknack that they might better explain.

"We're going camping with grandpa on Star Island."

"Where's that you're going?" asked a farmer who had just come out of the store after buying some groceries.

"Camping on Star Island in Clover Lake," repeated Ted.

"Huh! I wouldn't go there if I were you," said the farmer, shaking his head.

"Why not?" asked Ted. "Is it because of the blue light?" and he looked at his sister to see if she remembered.

"I don't know anything about a blue light," the farmer answered. "But if I were your grandfather I wouldn't take you there camping," and the man again shook his head.

"Why not?" asked Janet, her eyes opening wide in surprise.

"Well, I'll tell you why," went on the farmer. "I was over on Star Island fishing the other day, and I saw a couple of tramps, or maybe gypsies, there. I didn't like the looks of the men, and that's why I wouldn't go there camping if I were you or your grandpa," and the farmer shook his head again as he unhitched his team of horses.

CHAPTER III

OFF TO STAR ISLAND

"OH Ted!" exclaimed Janet, as she drove home in the goat-wagon with her brother and Baby William, "do you s'pose we can't go camping with grandpa?"

"Why can't we?" demanded Teddy.

" 'Cause of what that farmer said."

"Oh, well, I guess grandpa won't be 'fraid of tramps on the island. It's part his, anyhow, and he can make 'em get off."

"Yes, he could do that," agreed Janet, after thinking the matter over. "But if they were gypsies?"

"Well, gypsies and tramps are the same. Grandpa can make the gypsies get off the island too."

"They—they might take Trouble," faltered Jan in a low voice.

"Who?" asked Ted.

"The gypsies."

"Who take me?" demanded Trouble himself. "Who take me, Jam?"

Sometimes he called his sister Jam instead of Jan.

"Who take me?" he asked, playfully poking his fingers in his sister's eyes.

"Oh—nobody," she answered quickly, as she took him off her lap and put him behind her in the cart. She did not want to frighten her little brother. "Let's hurry home and tell grandpa," Jan said to Ted, and he nodded his curly head to show that he would do that.

On trotted Nicknack, Trouble being now seated in the back of the wagon on a cushion, while Ted and Jan were in front.

"Maybe it was tramps making a campfire that we saw last night," went on Jan after a pause, during which they came nearer to Cherry Farm.

"A campfire blaze isn't blue," declared Ted.

"Well, maybe this is a new kind."

Ted shook his head until his curls waggled.

"I don't b'lieve so," he said.

"Bang! There, me shoot you!" suddenly cried Trouble, and Ted and Jan heard something fall with a thud on the ground behind them.

"Whoa, there!" cried Ted to Nicknack. "What are you shootin', Trouble baby?" he asked, turning to look at his little brother.

"Me shoot a bunny rabbit," was the answer.

"Oh, there *is* a little bunny!" cried Jan, pointing to a small, brown one that ran along under the bushes, and then came to a stop in front of the goat-wagon, pausing to look at the children.

"Me shoot him," said Trouble, laughing gleefully.

"What with?" asked Ted, a sudden thought coming into his mind.

"Trouble frow store thing at bunny," said the little boy. "It bwoke an' all white stuff comed out!"

"Oh, Trouble, did you throw grandma's soda at the bunny?" cried Jan.

"Yes, I did," answered Baby William.

"And it's all busted!" exclaimed Ted, as he saw the white powder scattered about on the woodland path. "We've got to go back to the store for some more. Oh, Trouble Martin!"

"I's didn't hurt de bunny wabbit," said

Trouble earnestly. "I's only make-be'ieve shoot him—bang!"

"I know you didn't hurt the bunny," observed Jan. "But you've hurt grandma's soda. Is there any left, Ted?" she asked, as her brother got out of the wagon to pick up the broken package.

"A little," he answered. "There's some in the bottom. I guess we'll go back to the store and get more. I want to ask that farmer again about the tramps on Star Island."

"No, don't," begged Jan. "Let's take what soda we have to grandma. Maybe it'll be enough. Anyhow, if we did go back for more Trouble might throw that out, too, if he saw a rabbit."

"That's so. I guess we'd better leave him when we go to the store next time. How'd he get the soda, anyhow?"

"It must have jiggled out of my lap, where I was holding it, and then it fell in the bottom of the wagon and he got it. He didn't know any better."

"No, I s'pose not. Well, maybe grandma can use this."

Teddy carefully lifted up the broken package of baking soda, more than half of which had spilled when Trouble threw it at the little brown rabbit. Baby William may have thought the package of soda was a white stone, for it was wrapped in a white paper.

"Well, I'm glad he didn't hit the little bunny, anyhow," said Jan. "Where is it?" and she looked for the rabbit.

But the timid woodland creature had hopped away, probably to go to its burrow and tell a wonderful story, in rabbit language, about having seen some giants in a big wagon drawn by an elephant—for to a rabbit a goat must seem as large as a circus animal.

"I guess Trouble can't hit much that he throws at," observed Ted, as he started Nicknack once more toward Cherry Farm.

"He threw a hair brush at me once and hit me," declared Jan.

"Yes, I remember," said Teddy. "Here, Trouble, if you want to throw things throw these," and he stopped to pick up some old acorns which he gave his little brother. "You can't hurt anyone with them."

Trouble was delighted with his new playthings, and kept quiet the rest of the way home tossing the acorns out of the goatwagon at the trees he passed.

Off to Star Island

Grandma Martin said it did not matter about the broken box of soda, as there was enough left for her need; so Ted and Jan did not have to go back to the store.

"But I'd like to ask that farmer more about the tramps on Star Island," said Ted to his grandfather, when telling what the man had said at the grocery.

"I'll see him and ask him," decided Grandpa Martin.

It was two days after this—two days during which the Curlytops had much fun at Cherry Farm—that Grandpa Martin spoke at dinner one afternoon.

"I saw Mr. Crittendon," he said, "and he told me that he had seen you Curlytops at the store and mentioned the tramps on Star Island."

"Are they really there?" asked Jan eagerly.

"Well, they might have been. But we won't let them bother us if we go camping. I'll make them clear out. Most of that island belongs to me, and the rest to friends of mine. They'll do as I say, and we'll clear out the tramps."

"I hope you will, Grandpa," said Janet.

"Did Mr. Crittendon say anything about

the queer blue light Jan and Ted saw?" asked Grandma Martin.

"No, he hadn't seen that."

"Where did the tramps come from? And is he sure they weren't gypsies?" asked Jan's mother.

"No, they weren't gypsies. We don't often see them around here. Oh, I imagine the tramps were the regular kind that go about the country in summer, begging their way. They might have found a boat and gone to the island to sleep, where no constable would trouble them.

"But we're not afraid of tramps, are we, Curlytops?" he cried, as he caught Baby William up in his arms and set him on his broad shoulder. "We don't mind them, do we, Trouble?"

"We frow water on 'em!" said Baby William, laughing with delight as his grandfather made-believe bite some "souse" off his ears.

"That's what we will! No tramps for us on Star Island!"

"When are we going?" asked Ted excitedly.

"Yes, when?" echoed Jan.

"In a few days now. I've got to get out

the tents and other things. We'll go the first of the week I think."

Ted and Jan could hardly wait for the time to come. They helped as much as they could when Grandpa Martin got the tents out of the barn, and they wanted to take so many of their toys and playthings along that there would have been no room in the boat for anything else if they had had their way.

But Mother Martin thinned out their collection of treasures, allowing them to take only what she thought would give them the most pleasure. Boxes of food were packed, and a little stove made ready to take along, for although a campfire looks nice it is hard to cook over.

Trouble got into all sorts of mischief, from almost falling out of the haymow once, to losing the bucket down the well by letting the chain unwind too fast. But a hired man caught him as he toppled off the hay in the barn, and Grandpa Martin got the bucket up from the well by tying the rake to a long pole and fishing deep down in the water.

At last the day came when the Curlytops were to go camping on Star Island. The boat was loaded with the tents and other things, and two or three trips were to be made half-way across the lake, for the island was about in the middle. Nicknack and his wagon were to be taken over and a small stable made for him under a tree not far from the big tent.

"All aboard!" cried Ted, as he and Jan took their places in the first boat. "All aboard!"

"Isn't this fun!" laughed Janet, who was taking care of Trouble.

"Dis fun," echoed the little chap.

"I'm sure we'll have a nice time," said Mother Martin. "And your father will like it when he, too, can camp out with us."

"I hope the tramps don't bother you," said Mr. Crittendon, who had come to help Grandpa Martin get his camping party ready.

"Oh, we're not afraid of them!" cried Ted.

"Well, be careful; that's all I've got to say," went on the farmer. "I'll let you have my gun, if you think you'll need it," he said to Grandpa Martin.

"Nonsense! I won't need it, thank you. I'm not afraid of a few tramps. Besides I sent one of my men over to the island yesterday, and he couldn't find a sign of a vag-

Off to Star Island

rant. If any tramps were there they've gone."

"Wa-all, maybe," said the farmer, with a shake of his head. "Good luck to you, anyhow!"

"Thanks!" laughed Grandpa Martin.

"All aboard!" called Ted once more.

Then Sam, the hired man, and Grandpa Martin began to row the boat.

The Curlytops were off for Star Island, to camp out with grandpa.

CHAPTER IV

OVERBOARD

"TROUBLE! sit still!" ordered Janet.

"Yes, Trouble, you sit still!" called Mother Martin, as the Curlytops' grandfather and his man pulled on the oars that sent the boat out toward the middle of the lake. "Don't move about."

"I wants to splash water."

"Oh, no, you mustn't do that! Splashing water isn't nice," said Baby William's mother.

" 'Ike drandpa does," Trouble went on, pointing to the oars which the farmer was moving to and fro. Now and then a little wave hit the broad blades and splashed little drops into the boat.

"Trouble want do that!" declared the little fellow.

"No, Trouble mustn't do that," said his mother. "Grandpa isn't splashing the water. He's rowing. Sit still and watch him."

Baby William did sit still for a little while, but not for very long. His mother held to the loose part of his blue and white rompers so he would not get far away, but, after a bit, she rather forgot about him, in talking to Ted and Jan about what they were to do and not to do in camp.

Suddenly grandpa, who had been rowing slowly toward Star Island, dropped his oars and cried:

"Look out there, Trouble!"

"Oh, what's the matter?" asked Mother Martin, looking around quickly.

"Trouble nearly jumped out of the boat," explained Grandpa Martin. "I just grabbed him in time."

And so he had, catching Baby William by the seat of his rompers and pulling him back on the seat from which he had quickly sprung up.

"What were you trying to do?" asked Mrs. Martin.

"Trouble want to catch fish," was the little fellow's answer.

"Yes! I guess a fish would catch *you* first!" laughed Ted.

"I'll sit by him and hold him in," offered Janet, and she remained close to her small brother during the remainder of the trip across the lake. He did not again try to lean far over as he had done when his grandfather saw him and grabbed him.

"Hurray!" cried Teddy, as he sprang ashore. "Now for the camp! Can I help put up the tents, Grandpa?"

"Yes, when it's time. But first we must bring the rest of the things over. We'll finish that first and put up the tents afterward. We have two more boatloads to bring."

"Then can't I help do that?"

"Yes, you may do that," said Grandpa Martin with a smile.

"Can't I come, too?" asked Janet. "I'm almost as strong as Teddy."

"I think you'd better stay and help me look after Trouble," said Mrs. Martin. "Nora will be busy getting lunch ready for us, which we will eat before the tents are up."

"Oh, then I can help at that!" cried Janet, who was eager to be busy. "Come on, Nora! Where are the things to eat, Mother? I'm hungry already!"

"So'm I!" cried Ted. "Can't we eat befcre we go back for the other boatload, Grandpa?"

"Yes, I guess so. You Curlytops can eat while Sam and I unload the boat. I'll call you Teddy, when I'm ready to go back."

"All right, Grandpa."

The tents were to be put up and camp made a little way up from the shore near the spot at which they had landed. Grandpa Martin took out of the boat the different things he had brought over, and stacked them up on shore. Parts of the tents were there, and things to cook with as well as food to eat. More things would be brought on the next two trips, when another of the hired men was to come over to help put up the tents and make camp.

"Oh, I just know we'll have fun here, camping with grandpa!" laughed Jan, as she picked up her small brother who had slipped and fallen down a little hill, covered with brown pine needles.

"Let's go and look for something," proposed Ted, when he had run about a bit and thrown stones in the lake, watching the water splash up and hundreds of rings chase each other toward shore.

"What'll we look for?" asked Janet, as

she took hold of Trouble's hand, so he would not slip down again.

"Oh, anything we can find," went on Ted. "We'll have some fun while we're waiting for grandpa to get out the things to eat."

"I want something to eat!" cried Trouble. "I's hungry!"

"So'm I—a little bit," admitted Jan.

"Maybe we could find a cookie—or something—before they get everything unpacked," suggested Teddy, and this was just what happened. Grandpa Martin had some cookies in a paper bag in his pocket. Grandma Martin had put them there, for she felt sure the children would get hungry before their regular lunch was ready on the island. And she knew how hungry it makes anyone, children especially, to start off on a picnic in the woods or across a lake.

"There you are, Curlytops!" laughed Grandpa Martin, as he passed out the molasses and sugar cookies. "Now don't drop any of them on your toes!"

"Why not?" Ted wanted to know.

"Oh, because it might break them—I mean it might break your cookies," and Grandpa Martin laughed again.

"Come now, we'll go and look for things,"

Overboard

proposed Ted, as he took a bite of his cookie, something which Jan and Trouble were also doing.

"What'll we look for?" Jan asked again.

"Oh, maybe we can find a cave or a den where a—where a fox lives," he said, rather stumbling over his words.

At first Ted had been going to say that perhaps they would look for a bear's den, but then he happened to remember that even talk of a bear, though of course there were none on Star Island, might scare his little brother and Jan. So he said "fox" instead.

"Is there a fox here?" Jan asked.

"Maybe," said Ted. "Anyhow, let's go off and look."

"Don't go too far!" called Grandpa Martin after them, as he started to unload the boat and get the camp in order. "And don't go too near the edge of the lake. I don't want you to fall in and have your mother blame me."

"No, we won't!" promised Ted. "Come on," he called to his little brother and sister. "Oh, there you go again!" he cried, as he saw Trouble stumble and fall. "What's the matter?" he asked.

"It's these pine needles. They're awfully slippery," answered Janet. "I nearly slipped down myself. Did you hurt yourself, Trouble?" she asked the little fellow.

He did not answer directly, but first looked at the place where he had fallen. He could easily see it, because the pine needles were brushed to one side. Then Baby William tried to turn around and look at the back of his little bloomers.

"No, I isn't hurted," he said.

Janet and Ted laughed.

"I guess maybe he thought he might have broken his leg or something," remarked Teddy. "Now come on and don't fall any more, Trouble."

But the little fellow was not quite ready to go on. He stooped over and looked at the ground where he had fallen.

"What's the matter?" asked Janet, who was waiting to lead him on, holding his hand so he would not fall.

"Maybe he lost something," said Teddy. "Has he got any pockets in his bloomers, Jan?"

"No, mother sewed 'em up so he wouldn't put his hands in 'em all the while—and his hands were so dirty they made his bloomers

Overboard 49

the same way. He hasn't any pockets."

"Then he couldn't lose anything," decided Ted. He was always losing things from his pockets, so perhaps he ought to know about what he was talking. "What is it, Trouble?" he asked, for the little fellow was still stooping over and looking carefully at the ground near the spot where he had fallen.

"I—I satted right down on him," said Trouble at last, as he picked up something from the earth. "I satted right down on him, but I didn't bust him," and he held out something on a little piece of wood.

"What's he got?" asked Ted.

"Oh, it's only an ant!" answered Janet. "I guess he saw a little ant crawling along, just before he fell, and he sat down on him. Did you think you'd hurt the little ant, Trouble?"

"I satted on him, but I didn't hurt him," answered the little boy. "He can wiggle along nice—see!" and he showed the ant, crawling about on the piece of wood. Perhaps the little ant wondered how in the world it was ever going to get back to the ground again.

"Put him down and come on," said Ted. "We want to find something before grandpa puts up the tent. Maybe we can find the den where the fox lives."

Trouble carefully put the little ant back on the ground.

"I satted on him, but I didn't hurted him," again said the little fellow, grunting as he stood up straight again. Janet took his hand and they followed Teddy off through the forest.

It was very pleasant in the woods on Star Island. The sun was shining brightly and the waters of the lake sparkled in the sun. The children felt glad and happy that they had come camping with their grandpa, and they knew that the best fun was yet to happen.

"Let's look around for holes now," said Teddy, after they had gone a little way down a woodland path.

"What sort of holes?" asked Janet.

"Holes where a fox lives," answered her brother. "If we could find a fox maybe we could tame it."

"Wouldn't it bite?" the little girl asked.

"Well, maybe a little bit at first, but not after it got tame," said Teddy. "Come on!"

They walked a little way farther, and then Jan suddenly cried:

"Oh, I see a hole!"

She pointed to one beneath the roots of a big tree.

"That's a fox den, I guess!" exclaimed Teddy. "We'll watch and see what comes out."

The children hid in the bushes where they could look at the hole in the ground. For some time they waited, and then they began to get tired. The Curlytops were not used to keeping still.

"I'm going to sneeze!" said Trouble suddenly, and sneeze he did. And just then a little brown animal bounced out from under a bush and ran into the hole.

"Oh, it's a bunny rabbit!" cried Janet. "He lives in that hole! Come on, Ted, let's walk. We've found out what it was. It isn't a fox, it's a bunny! Let's go and find something else on the island. Maybe we can find a big cave."

"And maybe we'll find out what that blue light was," cried Ted eagerly.

"I guess I don't want to look for that," remarked Jan slowly.

"Why not?"

" 'Cause don't you 'member what Hal said about there bein' ghosts on this island?" and Janet looked over her shoulder, though it was broad daylight.

"Pooh!" laughed her brother. "I thought you didn't believe in ghosts."

"I don't—but——"

"I'm not afraid!" declared Teddy. "And I'm going to look and see if I can't find the lost star that fell on the island."

"Grandpa said it all burned up."

"Well, maybe a little piece of it was left. Anyhow I'm going to look."

So they looked, but they found nothing like the blue light, and then Ted said he was hungry and wanted to eat.

Nora and Mrs. Martin had set out a little lunch for the children on top of a packing box, and the Curlytops and Trouble were soon enjoying the sandwiches and cake, while their grandfather and the hired man finished unloading the boat. In a little while Grandpa Martin called:

"All aboard, Teddy, if you're going back with me!"

"I'm coming!" was the answer. "I'm coming!"

It did not take Grandpa Martin long to pull back to the mainland in the boat which was empty save for himself and Ted. The lake was smooth, a little wind making tiny waves that gently lapped the side of the boat.

"I think we'd better bring Nicknack over this trip," said Grandpa Martin, when a second farm hand met him on shore and began to help load the boat for the second trip. "The sooner we get that goat over on the island the better I'll feel."

"Why, you're not afraid of him, are you?" asked the hired man whose name was George.

"No. But I don't know how easy it's going to be to ferry him over. He may start some of his tricks. So we won't put much in the boat this time. We'll leave plenty of room for the goat and the cart."

"Oh, Nicknack will be good," declared Ted. "I know he will. Won't you, Nicknack?" and he put his arms around his pet. The goat had been driven down near the dock whence the boat started for Star Island.

"Well, unharness him and we'll get him on board," said the farmer. "Then we'll see what happens next."

Nicknack made no fuss at all about being unharnessed. His wagon was first wheeled on the boat, which was a large one and broad. Then Ted started Nicknack toward the craft.

"Giddap!" cried Teddy to Nicknack. "We're going to camp on Star Island, and you can have lots of fun! Giddap!"

Nicknack stood still on the dock for a few seconds, and he seemed to be sniffing the boat and the water in which it floated. Then with a little wiggle of his funny, short tail, he jumped down in near his wagon, and began eating some grass which Ted had pulled and placed there for him.

"It's a sort of bait, like a piece of cheese in a mouse trap," remarked Ted, as he saw the goat nibbling. "Isn't he good, Grandpa?"

"He's good now, Teddy; but whether he'll be good all the way over is something I can't say. I hope so."

George put in the boat as much as could safely be carried, with the goat as a passenger, and then he and Grandpa Martin began rowing toward Star Island. At first everything went very well. Nicknack seemed a little frightened when the boat tipped and rocked, but Ted patted him and fed him more grass, which Nicknack liked very much.

"I knew he'd be good!" Teddy said, when they were almost at the island, and could see Jan waving to them. "I knew he'd like the boat ride, Grandpa."

"Yes, he seems to like it. Now if we———"

But just then something happened.

The wind suddenly blew rather hard, roughening the water and causing the boat to tip. Nicknack was jostled over against the wagon, and some water splashed on him.

"Baa-a-a-a-a!" bleated the goat.

Then, before anyone could stop him, he gave a leap over Teddy's head, and into the water splashed Nicknack.

The goat had leaped overboard into the deepest part of Clover Lake!

CHAPTER V

THE BAG OF SALT

"Oh! Oh!" cried Teddy. "Oh, there goes my nice goat! Catch him, Grandpa! Stop him!"

Grandpa Martin stopped rowing and looked in surprise at the goat. So did the hired man.

"Well, just look!" exclaimed George.

"Oh, he'll be drowned! He'll be drowned!" wailed Teddy, tears coming into his eyes, for he loved Nicknack. "He'll be drowned!"

Grandpa Martin rested his hands on the oars and looked into the water. Then he smiled.

"I guess you'd have hard work drowning that goat," he said. "He's swimming like a fish!"

"And right straight for Star Island!" added the hired man. "That's a smart goat

The Bag of Salt

all right! He knows where he wants to go, and the shortest way to get there!"

Surely enough Nicknack was swimming toward the island. When he jumped out of the boat he floundered a little in the water, and splashed some on Teddy. Then he struck out, paddling as a dog does with his front feet. Nicknack turned himself about until he was headed toward the island, and then he swam straight toward it.

"Oh, won't he drown, Grandpa?" asked Teddy.

"I don't believe so, my boy! I guess Nicknack knows more than we thought he did. Maybe he didn't like the way we rowed, or he may have wanted a bath. Anyhow he jumped overboard, but he'll be all right."

"See him go!" cried the hired man.

Nicknack was swimming quite fast. Of course a goat is not as good a swimmer as is a duck or a fish, but Ted's pet did very well. On shore were Nora, Mrs. Martin, Janet, Trouble, and the farm hand who had gone over in the first boatload. They were watching the goat swimming toward them.

"Did you throw him into the water, Teddy?" asked Janet, as soon as the boat was near enough so that talking could be heard.

"He jumped in," Ted answered. "Isn't he a good swimmer?"

"I should say so! Here, Nicknack! Come here!" Janet called.

The goat, which had been headed toward a spot a little way down the island from where Janet and her mother stood, turned at the sound of the little girl's voice and came in her direction.

"Oh, he knows me!" she cried in delight. "Now don't shake yourself the way Skyrocket does, and get me all wet!" she begged, as Nicknack scrambled out on shore, water dripping from his hairy coat.

But the goat did not act like a dog, who gives himself a great shaking whenever he comes on shore after having been in the water. Nicknack just let it drip off him, and began to nibble some of the grass that grew on the island. He was making himself perfectly at home, it seemed.

The goat-wagon and the other things were soon landed, and then Grandpa Martin and one of the hired men went back for the last load. When that came back and the things were piled up near the tents, the work of set-

The Bag of Salt 59

ting up the camp went on. There was much yet to be done.

Ted and Jan helped all they could in putting up the tents. So did Mother Martin and Nora, who was large and strong. She could pull on a rope about as well as a man, and there were many ropes that needed tightening and fastening around pegs driven into the ground so the tents would not blow over in the wind.

Nicknack had been tied to a tree, near which, a little later, Ted and Jan were going to make him a little bower of leaves and branches. That was to be his stable until a better one could be built by Grandpa Martin —one that would keep Nicknack dry when it rained.

At last the tents were up, one for sleeping, another for cooking, and a third where the Curlytops and the others would eat their meals. It was a fine camp that Grandpa Martin made, and he knew just how to do it right, even to digging little trenches, or ditches, around the tents so the water would run off when it stormed.

"And now let's take a walk and see what we can find," suggested Ted to Janet, when Mother Martin said they might play about until supper was ready, for they had called the lunch they had eaten their dinner.

"Don't go too far," cautioned Mother Martin.

"Oh, we can't get lost on this island," said Ted. "All we'd have to do, if we were, would be to walk along the shore until we came to this camp."

"I know that. But it wasn't so much about your getting lost that I was thinking," said Mrs. Martin.

"Oh, you mean—the tramps?" half whispered Janet.

"Well, I don't know whether there are any here or not," went on her mother. "But it's best to be careful until grandpa has had a chance to look about. Where is grandpa now?"

"He's getting some water at the spring," Ted answered.

There was a fine spring on Star Island, not far from the place where the tents had been set up, and Mr. Martin was now bringing pails of water from that and pouring them into a barrel which would hold so much that even Trouble would have plenty to drink no matter how thirsty he was.

"Well, don't go too far away until either

grandpa or I have a chance to go with you," added Mrs. Martin.

"Me come, too," called Trouble, as he saw his brother and sister starting off.

"Oh, Mother!" exclaimed Teddy.

"No, you stay with mother," said Mrs. Martin. "I'll give you a nice drink of milk."

"Don't want milk. I's had milk. Trouble want Ted an' Jan."

"But you can't go with them, my dear. Come on, we'll go and throw stones into the lake and make-believe it's a great, big ocean!"

Baby William pouted a little at first. He liked to have his own way. But when he saw what fun his mother was having tossing stones into the lake and making the water splash up, Trouble did the same, laughing at the fun he was having.

"Dis a ocean, Momsey?" he asked as he set a little stick afloat, making believe it was a boat.

"Well, we'll call it an ocean," Mrs. Martin answered. "But this water is fresh, and that in the ocean is very salty. Some day I'll take you and my two little Curlytops to the real ocean, and you can taste how salty the waves are. Now we'll throw some more stones."

Meanwhile Ted and Jan started for a little walk down the path that went the whole length of Star Island.

"Shall we take Nicknack?" asked Jan.

"No, let's wait until he dries off after his bath," decided Teddy. "I don't like wet goats."

"Why, Teddy Martin! Nicknack got dried out hours ago!"

"Well, anyway, a goat isn't like a dog. We don't want a goat along when we are going out walking."

So Nicknack was left to nibble the grass, while the Curlytops wandered on and on. Grandpa and the hired men, having finished putting up the tents, were getting the stove ready so Nora could get supper.

"What are you looking for?" asked Jan when she noticed that her brother walked along as if searching for something. "Are you trying to see if any tramps or gypsies are here on the island?"

"No. I was thinking maybe I could find that fallen star."

"But didn't grandpa say it all melted up?"

The Bag of Salt

"Maybe a piece of it's left," went on Ted. This was the second time that he had spoken of the star that day. "If I can't find a chunk of it, maybe I can find the hole it made when it hit," he added. "I'd like to find that. Maybe it would be bigger than the one I dug when I thought I could go all the way through to China."

"Yes. The time Skyrocket fell in!" laughed Jan. " 'Member that, Teddy?"

"I guess I do! Daddy had to go out in the night and bring him in. Come on, let's look for the hole the shooting star made."

"All right."

The two Curlytops walked on over the island, looking here and there for star-holes. They found a number of deep places, but after looking at them, and poking sticks down into them, Ted decided that none of them had ever held a shooting star.

"Maybe bears made them," half whispered Jan.

"There aren't any bears on this island!" Teddy declared.

"I hope not," murmured his sister, as she looked over her shoulder and then kept close to her brother during the rest of the walk.

Pretty soon the children heard their

mother's voice calling them. They could hear very plainly, for the air was clear.

"I guess supper is ready," said Janet.

"I hope it is!" sighed Ted. "I'm awful hungry!"

Supper was ready, smoking hot on the table in the dining-tent, when Ted and Jan reached the camp grandpa had made.

"Oh, how good it smells!" cried Ted.

"And how nice the white tents look under the green trees," added his sister. "I just love it here!"

"It is the nicest place we have yet been for the summer vacation," said Mother Martin. "This and Cherry Farm are two lovely places."

They sat down under the tent and began to eat. Nora had gotten up a fine supper, for a regular cook stove had been brought along, and it was almost like eating at Grandma Martin's table, only this was out of doors, for the sides of the tent were raised to let in the air and the rays of the setting sun.

"What's the matter, Father?" asked Mrs. Martin, as she saw the children's grandfather pause after tasting the potatoes. "Is anything wrong?"

The Bag of Salt

"I think I'd like a little more salt on these."

"Yes, they do need salting. Nora, bring the salt please."

"There isn't any, except what I used when I was cooking—a little I had in a salt-shaker."

"Oh, yes, there must be. I brought a whole bagful. I saw it when I unpacked some of the things. There was a sack of salt."

"Well, it isn't here now," said Nora, as she looked among her kitchen things.

"Has anyone seen the bag of salt?" asked Mrs. Martin.

She looked at Ted and Jan, who shook their heads. Then Trouble's mother looked at him. He was busy with a piece of bread and jam. One could have told Trouble had been eating bread and jam just by looking at his mouth and face.

"Did you see the salt, Trouble?" asked his mother.

"Iss, I did," he answered, taking another bite.

"Where is it?"

"In de water," he replied. "I puts it in de water."

"You put the salt in the water? What water? Tell mother, Trouble."

"I puts salt in de lake water to make him 'ike ocean. Trouble 'ike ocean. Come on, I show!" and, getting down out of his chair, he toddled toward a little cove near the camp. The others, following him, saw something white on the ground near the edge of the lake. Grandpa Martin touched it with his finger and tasted.

"The little tyke did empty the whole bag of salt in the lake!" cried the farmer. "Fancy his trying to make it like the ocean! Ho! Ho!"

"Oh, Trouble!" cried Mrs. Martin. "You wasted a whole bag of salt, and now grandpa hasn't any for his potatoes!"

CHAPTER VI

TED AND THE BEAR

Baby William looked a little bit frightened and ashamed as his mother spoke to him in that way. He loved his grandfather, and of course he would not have done anything to make him feel bad if he had thought. But Trouble was a very little fellow, though his father often said he could get into as many kinds of mischief as could the larger Curlytops.

"Oh dear! This is too bad!" went on Mrs. Martin. "Why did you do it, Trouble? What made you empty the bag of salt into the lake?"

"Want to make ocean wif salt water," was the answer.

"I suppose it's my fault, for telling him so much about the big sea and its salt water," said Trouble's mother. "He liked to hear me talk about the ocean, and I guess he must have been thinking about it more than I had any idea of.

"He must have tasted the water of the lake, and found it wasn't salty, and then he thought that, to make an ocean and big waves out of a lake, all he had to do was to put in the salt. I'm sorry, Father."

"Oh, that's all right," laughed Grandpa Martin. "I guess I can get along without any more salt."

"Trouble sorry, too," said the little fellow, when he understood that he had done something wrong. "Me get salt water for you," and he started toward the place where he had emptied the bag into the water, carrying a spoon from the table.

"No, Trouble! Come back!" ordered his mother. "I guess he wants to dip up some salt water for you," she said laughingly to the children's grandfather, "but he'd be more likely to fall in himself."

She caught Trouble up in her arms and kissed him, and then Nora managed to find a little salt in the bottom of the shaker, so Grandpa Martin had some on his potatoes after all. But Trouble was told he must never again do anything like that.

He promised, of course, but Jan said:

Ted and the Bear

"He'll do something else, just as bad."

"I guess he will," laughed Teddy.

Supper over, Mr. Martin took his two men over to the mainland. On his return they all gathered about a little campfire grandpa made in front of the sleeping tent. The cot beds had been set up, and a mosquito netting was hung at the "front door" of the white canvas house, though really there was no door, just two flaps of the tent that could be tied together. But the netting kept out the bugs. Fortunately there were no mosquitoes, though all sorts of moths, snapping bugs and other flying things came around whenever a lantern was lighted.

"Tell us a story, Grandpa!" begged Janet, when they had finished talking about the many things that had happened during the first day in camp.

"Tell us about the shooting star that fell on this island," begged Teddy.

"Tell us about de twamps!" exclaimed Trouble, who ought to have been asleep, but who had begged to stay up a little longer than usual.

"I don't know anything about the tramps," laughed grandpa, "and I don't believe there are any on the island, though it is a large one, and it will take two or three days for us to walk all about it.

"As for the shooting star, which Teddy thinks about so much, I really didn't see it fall, and all I know is what the old men in the village have told me. It was many years ago."

"And did you ever see the blue light?" asked Ted, thinking of what he and his sister had seen the night they were coming home from the little visit to Hal Chester.

"No, I never did; though I'd like to, so I might know what it was."

"Children, how is grandpa ever going to tell you a story if you keep asking him so many questions?" laughed Mrs. Martin.

"All right—now we'll listen," promised Teddy, and Grandpa Martin told a tale of when he was a little boy, and lived further to the north and on the edge of a big wood where there were bears and other wild animals. His father was a good hunter, Grandpa Martin said, and often used to kill bears and wolves, for the country was wild, with never so much as one automobile in it.

Grandpa finished his story of the olden days by telling of once when he was a small boy, coming home through the woods toward dark one evening and being chased by a bear. But he crawled into a hollow log where the bear could not get him, and later his father and some other hunters came, shot the bear and got the little boy safely out.

"Whew!" whistled Teddy, when this was finished. "I'd like to have been there!"

"In the log, hiding away from the bear?" asked his mother.

"No, I—I guess not that," Ted answered. "I'd just like to have seen it up in a tree, where the bear couldn't get me."

"Bears can climb trees," remarked Janet.

"Well, I'd go up in a little tree too small for a bear," her brother answered.

"I guess you'd all better go to your little beds!" laughed Mother Martin. "It's long past your sleepy time."

And the Curlytops and Trouble were soon sound asleep.

It must have been about the middle of the night—anyhow it was quite late—when Teddy, who was sleeping in his cot next to one of the side walls of the tent, was suddenly awakened by a noise outside, and something seemed to be trying to get through.

"Oh! Oh!" cried Teddy, quickly sitting

up in bed, and wide awake all at once. "Oh, Mother! Something's after me! It's a bear! It's a bear!"

"Hush!" quickly exclaimed Mrs. Martin. "You'll waken William, and frighten him!"

"But Mother! I'm sure it's a bear! He growled!"

"What is it?" asked Jan, from her cot on the other side of the tent.

"It's a bear!" cried Ted again.

There did seem to be something going on outside the tent near Ted's side. There was a crackling in the bushes, and once something came pushing hard against the side of the white canvas house with force enough to make a bulge in it. Teddy jumped up from his cot and ran over to his mother, who was sitting up on her bed.

"Oh, Mother! It's coming in!" cried Teddy.

"Nonsense!" and Mrs. Martin laughed as she put her arms around her small son.

"What is it?" asked Grandpa Martin from the curtained-off part of the tent where he slept.

"It's a bear!" cried Janet.

Just then, from outside came a loud:

"Baa-a-a-a-a!"

Teddy looked very much surprised. Then he smiled. Then he laughed and cried:

"Why, it's our goat Nicknack!"

"I guess that's what it is," added Grandpa Martin. "But he seems to be in trouble. I'll go outside and look."

Taking a lantern with him, while Mrs. Martin and the children waited a bit anxiously, Grandpa Martin went to see what had happened. The Curlytops heard him laughing as they saw the flicker of his light through the white tent. Then they heard Nicknack bleating again. The goat seemed, to those inside, to be kicking about with his little black hoofs.

"Whoa there, Nicknack!" called Grandpa Martin. "I'll soon get you loose!"

There was more noise, more tramping in the bushes and then, after a while, Grandpa Martin came back.

"What was it?" asked Ted and Jan in whispers, for their mother had begged them not to awaken Trouble, who was still sleeping peacefully.

"It was your goat," was the answer. "He had got loose, and his horns were caught between two trees where he had tried to jump. He was held fast by his horns and he was kicking his heels up in the air, trying to get loose."

"Did you get him out?" asked Jan.

"Yes, I pried the trees apart and got his head loose. Then he was all right. I tied him good and tight in his stable, and I guess he won't bother us again to-night."

"Then it wasn't a bear after all," remarked Jan, laughing at her brother.

"No, indeed! There aren't any bears on this island," said her grandfather. "Go to sleep."

Nothing else happened the rest of the night, and they all slept rather late the next morning, for they were tired from the work of the day before. The sun was shining over Clover Lake when Nora rang the breakfast bell, and Ted and Jan hurried with their dressing, for they were eager to be at their play.

"What'll we do to-day?" asked Janet, as she tried to get a comb through her thick, curly hair.

"We'll go for a ride with Nicknack," decided Ted, who was also having a hard time with his locks. "Oh, I wish I was a barber!" he cried, as the comb stuck in a bunch of curls.

"Why?" asked his mother, who was giving Trouble his breakfast.

" 'Cause then I'd cut my own hair short, and I'd never have to comb it."

"Oh, I wouldn't want to see you without your curls," Mother Martin said. "Here, I'll help you as soon as I feed Trouble."

Trouble could feed himself when his plate had been set in front of him, and while he was eating Mrs. Martin made her two Curlytops look better by the use of their combs.

After breakfast the children ran to hitch Nicknack to the wagon. Grandpa Martin was going back in the rowboat to the mainland to get a few things that had been forgotten, and also another bag of salt.

"And I'll hide it away from Trouble," said Nora with a laugh. "We don't want any more salty oceans around here."

"Let's drive away before Trouble sees us," proposed Jan to her brother. "He'll want to come for a ride and we can't go very far if he comes along."

"All right. Stoop down and walk behind the bushes. Then he can't see us."

Jan and Ted managed to get away unseen, and were soon hitching their goat to the wagon. Trouble finished his breakfast and called to them, wanting to go with them wherever they went. But his mother knew the two Curlytops did not want Trouble with them every time, so Baby William had to play by himself about camp, while the two older children drove off on a path that led the long way of the island.

"Maybe we'll have an adventure," suggested Jan, as she sat in the cart driving the goat, for she and her brother took turns at this fun.

"Maybe we'll see some of the tramps," he added.

"I don't want to," said Jan.

"Well, maybe we'll see a bear."

"I don't want that, either. I wish you wouldn't say such things, Teddy."

"Well, what do you want to see?"

"Oh, something nice—flowers or birds or maybe a fairy."

"Huh! I guess there's no fairies on this island, either. Let's see if we can find an apple tree. I'd like an apple."

"So would I. But we mustn't eat green ones."

"Not if they're too green," agreed Teddy. "But a little green won't hurt."

They drove on, Nicknack trotting along

the path through the woods, now and then stopping to nibble at the leaves. At last the children came to a beautiful shady spot, where many ferns grew beneath the trees, and it was so cool that they stopped their goat, tied him to an old stump and sat down to eat some cookies their mother had given them. The Curlytops nearly always became hungry when they were out on their little trips.

"Wouldn't it be funny," remarked Ted, after a bit, "if we should see a bear?"

"The-o-dore Martin!" gasped Janet. "I wish you'd keep quiet! It makes me scared to hear you say that."

"Well, I was only foolin'," and Teddy dropped a "g," a habit of which his mother was trying to break him. And he did not often forget.

"If I saw a bear," began Janet, "I'd just scream and——"

Suddenly she stopped because of a queer look she saw on her brother's face. Teddy dropped the cookie he had been about to bite, and, pointing toward a hollow log that lay not far off, said, in a hoarse whisper:

"Look, Jan! It *is* a bear!"

CHAPTER VII

JAN SEES SOMETHING

For a moment after her brother had said this Janet did not speak. She, too, dropped the cookie she had just taken from the bag, and turned slowly around to see at what Teddy was pointing.

She was just in time to see something furry and reddish-brown in color dart into the hollow log, which was open at both ends. Then Jan gave a scream.

"Oh!" exclaimed Ted, who was as much frightened by Janet's shrill voice as he was at what he had seen. "Oh, Jan! Don't!"

"I—I couldn't help it," she answered. "I told you I'd scream if I saw a bear, and I *did* see one. It is a bear, isn't it, Teddy?"

"It is," he answered. "I saw it first. It's my bear!"

"You can have it—every bit of it," said Jan, quickly getting up from the mossy rock on which she had been sitting. "I don't want any of it, not even the stubby tail. I like to own half of Nicknack with you, but I don't want half a bear."

"Then I'll take all of it—it's my bear," went on Ted. "Where're you going, Jan?" he asked, as he saw his sister hurrying away.

"I'm going home. I don't like it here. I'm going to make Nicknack run home with me."

Teddy got up, too. He did not stop to pick up the cookie he had dropped.

"I—I guess I'll go with you, Jan," he said. "I guess my bear will stay in the log until I come back."

"Are you coming back?" asked Janet, as with trembling fingers she unfastened Nicknack's strap from around the stump to which he had been tied.

"I'm going to get grandpa to come back with me and shoot the bear," replied Ted. "I want his skin to make a rug. You know —like grandpa did with the bear his father shot."

Jan did not say anything. She got into the cart and turned the goat about, ready to leave the place. She gave a look over her shoulder at the hollow log into which she and

Ted had seen the furry, brown animal crawl. It did not seem to be coming out, and Jan was glad of that.

"Giddap, Nicknack!" she called to the goat, and as the animal started off Ted jumped into the wagon from behind.

"I wish I had a gun," he said.

"You're too little," declared Jan. "Oh, Ted! what if he should chase us? Was it an awful big bear? I didn't dare look much."

"It wasn't so very big."

"Was it as big as Nicknack?"

"Oh, bigger'n him—a lot."

"Oh!" and again Jan looked back over her shoulder. "I hope he doesn't chase us," she added.

"I'll fix him if he does!" threatened Ted. "I'll fix him!"

"How? You haven't any gun, and maybe you couldn't shoot it if you had, lessen maybe it was your Christmas pop gun."

"Pooh! Pop guns wouldn't be any good to shoot a bear! You've got to have real bullets. But I can fix this bear if he chases us," and Ted tried to look brave.

"How?" asked Jan again. She felt safer now, for Nicknack was going fast, and the hollow log, into which the furry animal had crawled, was out of sight.

"I'll make our goat buck the bear with his horns if he chases us, that's what I'll do!" declared Ted.

"Oh, that would be good!" exclaimed Jan in delight. "Nicknack is brave and his horns are sharp. 'Member how he stuck 'em in the fence one day?"

"Yes," answered Ted, "I do. And I'll get him to stick 'em in the bear if he comes too close. Giddap, Nicknack!" and Ted flicked the goat with the ends of the reins. I think he wanted the goat to go faster so there would be no danger of the bear's chasing after him and his sister. Perhaps Ted thought Nicknack might be afraid of the bear, even if the goat did have sharp horns.

The Curlytops were greatly excited when they reached the camp. Trouble was playing out in front and Grandpa Martin had just landed in the boat.

"What's that?" he cried, when he heard Ted's story. "A bear in a hollow log? Nonsense! There are no bears on Star Island."

"But I saw it, and so did Janet. Didn't you, Jan?" cried Ted.

"I saw something fuzzy with a big tail

going inside the log," answered Teddy's sister.

"Then it couldn't have been a bear," laughed Grandpa Martin. "For a bear has only a little short, stubby tail. I'll go to see what it is. I think I know, however."

"What?" asked Mother Martin. "Don't go into any danger, Father."

"I won't," promised the farmer. "But I won't tell you what I think the animal is until I see it. I may be mistaken."

"Maybe it's a twamp," put in Trouble, who seemed to be thinking about them as much as Ted thought about the fallen star.

"Tramps aren't animals," laughed Jan.

"Furry animals, anyway," added Ted.

"Well, you stay here and I'll go see what it was," went on grandpa, and he started off toward the hollow log with a big club. He was not gone very long, and when he came back he was laughing, as he had the night before when Nicknack gave them a scare.

"Just as I thought!" cried the children's grandpa. "It was a big, red fox in the hollow log."

"And not a bear?" asked Ted.

"Not a bear, Curlytop! Only a fox that was more frightened by you than you were

Jan Sees Something

by him, I guess. I knew it couldn't be a bear."

"How did you get it out of the log?" asked Jan.

"Oh, I just tapped on the log with my club, and Mr. Fox must have thought it was somebody knocking at his front door. For out he ran, looked at me with his bright eyes, and then away he ran into the woods. So you Curlytops needn't be afraid. The fox won't hurt you."

"I'm glad of that," said Jan. "Now let's go fishing, Ted."

"All right," he agreed.

"Can't you take Trouble with you?" asked his mother. "I want to help Nora and grandpa do a little work around the camp."

"Yes, we'll take him," agreed Jan. "But you mustn't put any salt in the water, Trouble, and scare the fish."

"I not do it. I tatch a fiss myself."

They gave him a pole and a line without any hook on it so he could not scratch himself, and then Jan and Ted sat down under a shady tree, not far from camp, to try to catch some fish.

They knew how, for their father had taught them, and soon Jan had landed a good-sized sunfish. A little later Ted caught a perch which had stripes on its sides, "like a zebra," as Jan said. After that Jan and Ted each caught two fish, and they soon had enough to cook.

"What do you Curlytops want me to do with these?" asked Nora, as the two children came along, laughing and shouting, with the fish dangling from strings each of them carried.

"Cook 'em, of course!" cried Teddy. "That's what we caught them for, Nora—to have you cook them."

"But won't they bite me?" asked the cook, pretending to be afraid.

"Oh, no! They can't!" explained Jan.

"They bit on our hooks, and now they can't bite any more, but we can bite them," said Teddy.

"Oh, would you bite the poor fish?" asked Nora.

For a moment the Curlytops did not know what to answer. Then Teddy replied:

"Oh, well, it can't hurt 'em to bite 'em after they're cooked, can it?"

"No, I guess not," laughed Nora, "no more than it can hurt a baked potato. Well, run along and I'll get the fish ready for

Jan Sees Something

dinner, or whatever you call the next meal. I declare, I'm so mixed up with this camping business that I hardly know breakfast from supper. But run along, and I'll fry the fish for you, anyhow."

"Let's go and take a walk," proposed Jan, when they had washed their hands in the tin basin that Mother Martin had set on a bench under a tree, with a towel and soap near by, for fish did leave such a funny smell on your hands, the little girl said.

"Where'll we walk to?" asked Teddy.

"Oh, let's go and look. Maybe we can find that cute little bunny we saw when we were looking for the den where the fox lived but didn't find him," proposed Jan.

"All right," answered Teddy, and they set off.

They had not gone very far before Teddy stopped near a bush and began to look about him.

"What's the matter?" asked his sister.

"Why, I saw a bird fly out of here," answered her brother, "and it seemed just as if it had a broken wing. It couldn't fly—hardly."

"Where is it?" asked Jan eagerly. "Maybe if we take it to mother she can fix the wing. Once she mended a dog's broken leg, and he could walk 'most as good as ever when he got well, only he limped a little."

"But a dog can't fly," said Teddy.

"I know it," agreed Jan. "But if mother can mend a broken leg, she can fix a broken wing, can't she?"

"Maybe," admitted her brother. "Oh, there's the bird again, Jan! See how it flutters along!" and the little boy pointed to one that was dragging itself along over the ground as though its wings or legs were broken or hurt.

"Come on!" cried Teddy. "Maybe we can catch the bird, Jan!"

Brother and sister started after the little feathered songster, which was making a queer, chirping noise. Then Jan suddenly called:

"Oh, here's another!"

And, surely enough, there was a second bird acting almost as was the first—fluttering along, half hopping and half flying through the grass.

"We'll get 'em both!" yelled Teddy, and he and Jan hurried along. But, somehow or other, as soon as they came almost to the place where they could reach out and touch one of the birds, which acted as though it could not go a bit farther, the little creature would manage to flutter on just beyond the eager hands of the children.

"That's funny!" exclaimed Teddy. "I almost had one of 'em that time!"

"So did I!" added Janet. "Now I'm sure I can get this one!" and she ran forward to grasp the fluttering bird, but it managed to hop along, just out of her reach.

The one Ted was after did the same thing, and for some time the children hurried on after the birds. At last the two songsters, with little chirps and calls, suddenly flew high in the air and circled back through the woods.

"Well, would you look at that!" cried Teddy, in surprise.

"They can fly, after all!" gasped Janet. "What d'you s'pose made 'em pretend they couldn't?"

"I—I guess they wanted to fool us," said her brother.

And that really was it. The little birds had built a nest in a low bush, close to the ground where the children could easily have reached it if they had seen it. And they were very close to it, though their eyes had not spied it.

But the birds had seen the Curlytops and, fearing that Jan and Ted might take out the eggs in the nest, the wise little birds had pretended to be willing to let the boy and girl catch them instead of robbing the nest.

Of course, Jan and Ted wouldn't have done such a thing as that! But the birds knew no differently. Not all birds act this way—pretending to be hurt, or that they can't fly—to get people to chase after them, and so keep far away from the little nests. But this particular kind of bird always does that.

Some day, if you are in the woods or the fields, and see one bird—or two—acting in this queer way, as though it could not fly or walk, and as though it wanted you to hurry after it and try to catch it—if you see a bird acting that way you may be sure you are near its nest and eggs and this is the way the bird does to get you away.

"Let's look for their nest," suggested Teddy, when the two birds had flown far away, back through the woods.

"Oh, no," answered Jan. "We don't want to scare them. Maybe we can look a

Jan Sees Something

the nest of a bird that won't mind if we watch her feeding her little ones."

And, a little later, they came to a bush in which was a robin's nest. In it were some tiny birds, and, by standing on their tiptoes, and bending the nest down a little way, the Curlytops could look in. The baby birds, which had only just begun to grow feathers, opened their mouths as wide as they could, thinking, I suppose, that Jan and Ted had worms or bugs for them.

But the children did not have.

"Your mother will soon be along to feed you," said Janet, and soon the mother bird did come flying back from the field. She seemed afraid at first, when she saw how close Jan and Ted were to her nest, but the children soon walked away, and then the robin fed her young.

Ted and Jan had a nice walk through the woods and then they went back to camp.

"We'll take Trouble for a walk, so mother won't have to look after him so much," said Janet. "Come, Trouble!"

"Show me where the fox was," begged Baby William, and Ted and Jan turned their steps that way. But there was no sign of the big-tailed animal in the hollow log, though the children pounded on it as Grandpa Martin said he had done.

Then they wandered on a little farther in the beautiful woods. Jan saw some flowers she wanted to gather, and leaving the path where Ted stood to take care of his little brother, she began picking a handful.

Janet saw so many pretty blossoms that she went a little farther than she meant to, and, before she knew it, she had lost sight of her two brothers, though she could hear them talking.

Suddenly, after crawling through some bushes, Jan found herself on another path. On the other side of it she saw some black-eyed Susans.

"Oh, I must get some of them!" she cried.

She darted across the path, and, as she was about to pick the flowers, she saw, standing behind a big tree, a man who had on very ragged clothes. He looked at Jan, who dropped her bouquet and gasped:

"Oh! Oh, dear!"

The ragged man looked at Janet and smiled. But Jan did not smile. One thought only was in her mind.

"Here is one of the tramps!"

CHAPTER VIII

TROUBLE FALLS IN

JANET MARTIN thought it must have been all of five minutes that she stood staring at the ragged man and he at her, though, very likely, it was only a few seconds. A little while seems very long sometimes; for instance, waiting for a train, or for the day of the party to come.

"Are you looking for anything?" the man asked of Janet after a while.

"He doesn't speak like a tramp," thought the little girl, who had occasionally heard them asking Nora, at the back door at home, for something to eat. "I guess I'll answer him."

So she replied:

"I'm looking for flowers."

"Well, there are some pretty ones here in the woods," went on the ragged man. "I saw some fine red ones a little while ago. If

I had known I should meet you I would have picked them for you."

"I wonder if he *can* be a tramp," thought Janet. "Do tramps pick flowers, or want to pick them?"

What she said was:

"Thank you, but I think I have enough now."

"Yes, you have a nice bouquet," went on the ragged man, still smiling.

He was dressed like a tramp, that was certain. But, somehow or other, Janet did not feel as afraid as she expected she would be when she thought of meeting a tramp.

"Do you live around here?" the man continued.

"Yes, we're camping in a tent," Jan replied. "My grandfather owns part of this island and we're with him—my mother and my brothers. We like it here."

"Yes, it's fine," said the ragged man, who Janet thought must be a tramp, even if he did not talk like most of them. "So you live in a tent? Does the professor stay here all the while?"

"The professor?" repeated Janet, and she wondered what the long word meant. She was sure she had heard it before.

"HERE IS ONE OF THE TRAMPS!"

The Curlytops on Star Island Page 90

Pretty soon she remembered. At school she had heard some of the teachers speak of the principal as "Professor."

"My grandpa isn't a professor," explained Janet with a smile. "He's a farmer."

"Well, some farmers are scientists. Maybe he is a scientist," went on the tramp. "I was wondering if some one else was on this island looking for the same thing I'm looking for. Can you tell me, little girl——?"

But just then, from somewhere back in the woods, a voice called. The ragged man listened a moment, and then he cried:

"All right! I'm coming!"

Janet saw him stoop and pick up off the ground a canvas bag, through the opening of which she saw stones, such as might be picked up on the shore of the lake or almost anywhere on the island.

"I hope I shall see you again, little girl," went on the tramp, as Janet called him afterward when telling the story. "And when I do, I hope I'll have some red flowers for you. Good-bye!"

Janet was so surprised by the quick way in which the man ran off through the woods with his bag of stones that she did not answer or say good-bye. She just stood looking at the quivering bushes which closed up behind him and showed which way the man had gone. Janet could not see him any longer.

A moment later she heard the bushes behind her crackling, and, turning quickly, she saw Ted and Trouble coming toward her.

"What's the matter?" called her older brother. "Did you see another bear—I mean a fox?"

"No. But I saw a tramp man," replied Janet. "Oh, but he was awful ragged!"

"A tramp!" cried Ted. "Then we'd better get away from here. We'd better go and tell grandpa!"

Janet thought the same thing, and, after telling Ted all that had happened and what she and the man had said, the Curlytops hurried back through the woods to the camp.

"A ragged man on the island; is that it?" asked Grandpa Martin, when Jan told him what had happened. "It must be as Mr. Crittendon said, that there are tramps here. Though what they are doing I don't know. There isn't anything to eat here, except what we brought. And you haven't missed anything, have you, Nora? Has anybody been taking your strawberry shortcake or apple dumplings from the tent kitchen?"

"No, Mr. Martin, they haven't," Nora answered.

"Well, maybe it was a tramp and perhaps it wasn't," said Grandpa Martin. "Still it will be a good thing to have a look about the island. I don't want strange men roaming where they please, scaring the children."

"Oh, he didn't scare me, except at first," Janet hastened to say. "He spoke real nice to me, but his clothes were old and awful ragged. He wanted to know if you were a professor."

"Well, I guess I'm professor enough to drive away tramps that won't work, and only want to eat what other people get," returned the farmer. "I'll have a look around this island to-morrow, and drive away the tramps."

"And until then, don't you Curlytops go far away. Stay where I can watch you," went on Mrs. Martin, shaking her finger at them, half in fun, but a great deal in earnest.

"We'll stay near the tent," promised Jan.

"I'm going to help grandpa hunt the tramps," declared Ted.

"No, Curlytop, you'd better stay with your sister and mother," said the farmer. "I don't really believe there are any tramps here."

"But I saw him!" insisted Janet.

"I know you saw some one, Curly Girl," and grandpa smiled at her. "Of course there may be a strange man—maybe two, for you say you heard one call to the other. But they may have just stopped for a little while on this island. I'll have to ask them to go away, though, for we want to be by ourselves while camping. So, as there might be strangers around here who would not be pleasant, you'd better stay here, too, Teddy."

"All right, I'll stay," Teddy promised, and he tried to be happy and contented about it, though he did want to go with his grandfather on the "tramp-hunt" as he called it. But, though Teddy was quite a good-sized boy for his age, there were some things that it was not wise for him to do. This was one of them.

The next day Grandpa Martin, rowing over to the mainland, brought back with him one of his hired men. The two walked all over the island, only stopping for their lunch, and at night they had found no trace of anyone.

"If tramps were here they have gone," said Grandpa Martin. "I can't think why that man who talked to Janet should speak of a professor, though."

"It *is* queer," said Mrs. Martin. "Never mind, I'm glad it is safe for the children to run about now. It has been hard work to keep them about the tents all this day."

"I guess it has been," laughed Grandpa Martin. "Well, to-morrow they can run as much as they like."

Ted and Janet had lots of fun, playing on the shores of Clover Lake. They took off their shoes and stockings, and went wading. Trouble did the same, splashing about in his bare feet until he saw a little crawfish, darting from one stone to another under water to hide away.

"Trouble 'fraid of dem big water-bugs," he said, as he ran out on the grassy bank. "Don't want to wade any more," and Ted and Jan could not get him to come in again that day.

By this time the camp was well settled.

They had stored away in the cooking tent many good things to eat, and whenever they wanted anything more Grandpa Martin would row over to the store on the mainland for it.

Daddy Martin wrote from Cresco, where he was looking after his store, that he would soon be back at Cherry Farm, and then he would come out to the camp and spend a week.

The Curlytops played all the games they knew. They took long rides with Nicknack, and often Trouble went with them. But it was not all play. Mrs. Martin thought it wise for Ted and Jan to have some work to do; so, each day, she gave them little tasks. They had to bring a small pail of water from the spring, gather wood for the evening campfire, and also some for Nora to use when she made the fire in the cook-stove. For Nora was a good cook, and many a fine pie or cake came out of the oven. Sometimes Ted and Jan helped around the kitchen by drying the dishes or helping set the table or clear it off.

One afternoon, when it was almost time to get supper, Mrs. Martin sent Ted to the spring for a pail of water. She wanted one

Trouble Falls In 99

so they could all have a fresh drink, as it was rather warm that day.

"I'll go with you," offered Janet.

"Me come too," added Trouble.

"Yes, take him," said his mother to Janet. "He hasn't been out much to-day." So Trouble toddled off with his brother and sister.

Ted filled the pail at the bubbling spring, which was a large one, out of sight of the tents of the camp. Then he heard a strange bird whistling in a tree overhead, and, setting down the pail, he ran to see what it was.

"Oh, Jan," called her brother a moment later, "it's a big red and black bird. Awful pretty! Come and see him!"

Jan ran to get a look at the scarlet tanager, as grandpa said later it was, and, without thinking, she left Trouble alone.

Well, you can well imagine what Trouble did!

For a long while—ever since he had been in camp, in fact—Baby William had wanted to dip a pail of water out of the spring. But of course he could not be allowed to do this, for he might fall in. Now, however, he saw his chance.

"Trouble bring de water," he said, talking to himself while Teddy and Janet were looking at the pretty bird.

The little fellow carefully emptied the pail his brother had filled. Then with it in his hand he went slowly toward the spring. He leaned over, but longer arms than his were needed to reach the pail down into the bubbling water.

Trouble reached and stretched and reached again, and then——

"Splash!"

Baby William had fallen in!

CHAPTER IX

TED FINDS A CAVE

JANET and Ted returned from looking at the pretty scarlet bird just in time to see what happened to Trouble. They saw him fall into the spring.

"Oh!" cried Janet, clasping her hands. "Oh, look!"

"He'll be drowned!" yelled Ted, and then he ran as fast as he could toward the place where he had last seen his little brother, for Baby William was not in sight now. He was down in the water.

Perhaps Trouble might not have come to any harm, more than to get wet through by the time Ted reached him. Perhaps the little fellow might not have been drowned. At any rate, no harm came to him, even though Jan and her brother did not get there in time to help.

The two Curlytops, their fuzzy hair fluttering in the wind, were half way to the spring when they saw coming from the bushes a ragged man.

"There he is!" cried Janet.

"Who?" asked Ted.

"The man who—talked to me—while I was picking flowers," and Jan's voice came in gasps, for she was getting out of breath from having run so hard. "There he is!" and she pointed.

"That's the tramp!" cried Ted. "They *are* on the island, only grandpa couldn't find 'em!"

"Do you—do you s'pose he's goin' to take Trouble?" faltered Janet.

Before Ted could answer, the Curlytops saw what the ragged man was going to do. They saw him stoop over the spring, reach down into it and lift something up. The "something" was Baby William, screaming and crying in fright, and dripping wet.

The ragged man set Trouble down on a rock near the spring, and then, waving his hand to Ted and Jan, he cried:

"He's all right—swallowed hardly any water. Take him home as soon as you can, though. I haven't time to stop—have to go to see the professor!"

With that the man seemed to dive in between some high bushes, and the Curlytops could not see him any more. But Trouble was still sitting on the rock, the water from his clothes making a little puddle all around him, and he was crying hard, his tears running down his cheeks.

"Oh, Trouble!" gasped Jan, putting her arms around him, all wet as he was.

"Are you hurt?" asked Ted, looking carefully at his little brother.

"I—I—I fal—falled in an'—an' I's all—all wetted!" wailed Trouble, his breath coming in gasps because of his crying, which he had partly stopped on seeing his brother and sister. "I falled in de spwing, I did!"

"What made you?" asked Ted, while Jan tried to wring some of the water out of the little fellow's waist and rompers.

"I wanted to get de pail full for mamma."

"But I filled the pail, Trouble. You oughtn't to have touched it," said Teddy. He went to the spring and looked down in it. The pail was at the bottom of the little pool.

"It's a good thing that tramp got him out," remarked Janet. "He must be a nice man, even if his clothes are ragged."

"I guess so, too," agreed Ted. "But he said we must take Trouble home. I guess we'd better."

"Yes," assented Jan. "But he isn't hurt."

"He wasn't in very long," Ted said. "The man got him out awful quick—quicker than we could. You lead him home, Jan, and I'll get the pail out of the spring. It's sunk like a ship."

"How're you going to get it?"

"With a stick, I guess. You mustn't lean over the spring any more, Trouble."

"No," promised Baby William.

But the Curlytops could not be sure he would keep his promise. He might for a time, while he remembered what had happened to him.

With a crooked stick Teddy managed to fish up the pail after two or three trials. Then, filling it with water from the spring, he carried it back to camp, while Jan led the wet and dripping Trouble.

"Oh, my goodness! What's happened now?" asked Nora, as she saw the three children coming into camp. "Did you go in swimming with all your clothes on, Trouble?"

Ted Finds a Cave

"No. I falled into de spwing, I did!"

"And the tramp got him out!" added Jan.

Then she and Teddy, taking turns, told what had happened. Mrs. Martin scolded Trouble a little, to make him more careful the next time. Then Grandpa Martin said:

"Well, there must be strangers on this island after all, though I could not find them. They must be hiding somewhere, and I'd like to know what for."

"Maybe they're living in gypsy wagons," suggested Jan.

"Or in a cave," added Ted. "They look as if they lived in a cave."

"There isn't any cave on the island, as far as I know," his grandfather told Ted. "But I don't like those strange men roaming about our place here. They may not do any harm, but I don't like it. I'll have another look for them."

"So will I," added Teddy, but he did not say this aloud. Teddy had made up his mind to do something. He was going to look for those men himself, either in a cave or a gypsy wagon. Ted wanted to find the ragged man—find all of them if more than one; and there seemed to be at least two, for the one who had pulled Teddy out of the spring had spoken of another—a "professor."

"What's a professor?" asked Jan.

"Oh, it's a man or a woman who has studied his lessons and teaches them to others," answered her mother. "One who knows a great deal about something, such as about the stars or about the world we live in. Professors find out many things and then tell others — young people generally — about them."

"I'm going to be a professor," said Teddy.

"Are you?" inquired his mother with a smile. "I hope you will get wise enough to be one."

But Teddy did not speak all that was in his mind. If a professor was one who found out things, then the small boy decided he would be one long enough to find out about the tramps, and perhaps find the cave where they lived, and then he could tell Jan.

When Trouble had been put into dry clothes and sent to sleep by his mother's singing, "Ding-dong bell, Pussy's in the well," Jan and Ted sat by themselves, talking over what had happened that day. Ted was making a small boat to sail on the lake,

Ted Finds a Cave

and Jan was mending her doll's dress, where a prickly briar bush had torn a little hole in it.

Early the next morning Ted slipped away from his place at the breakfast table, and motioned to Jan to join him behind the sleeping tent. Ted held his finger over his lips to show his sister that he wanted her to keep very quiet.

"What's the matter?" she whispered, when they were safe by themselves. "Did you see the tramp-man?"

"No, but I'm going to find him!"

"You are?" cried Janet, and her eyes opened wide with wonder and surprise.

"Don't tell anybody," went on Ted. "We don't want Trouble to follow us. Come on off this way," and he pointed to a path that led through the bushes back of the tent.

Trouble was busy just then, playing in the sand on the shore of Clover Lake, while Mrs. Martin and Nora were clearing away the breakfast things. Grandpa Martin was raking up around the tents, so no one saw the Curlytops slip away.

"Which way are you going?" asked Jan of her brother.

"Over to the spring."

"What for? To get more water? Where's your pail?"

"I don't have to get water yet," answered Ted. "I'm going to the spring to look to see if I can tell which way that tramp went. Don't you know how Indians do—look at the leaves and grass in the woods, and they can tell by the marks which way anybody went? Mother read us a story once like that."

"I don't like Indians," remarked Jan somewhat shortly, half turning back.

"Oh, there's no Indians!" exclaimed Ted impatiently. "I was only sayin' what they did. Come on!"

So Jan followed her brother, though she was a little bit afraid. However, she saw nothing to frighten her, and it was nice in the woods. The wind was blowing through the trees, the birds were singing and it was cool and pleasant. The Curlytops soon came to the spring where Trouble had fallen in.

"Now we must look all around," declared Teddy.

"What for?" his sister demanded again.

"To tell which way the tramp-man went. Then we can find his cave."

"Maybe he lives in a wagon or a tent."

Ted Finds a Cave

"Then we'll find them. Come on, help look!"

"I don't know how," confessed Janet.

"Well, look for a place where the bushes are broken down and where you see footprints in the dirt. That's the way Indians tell. Mother read it out of a book to us."

So Jan and Ted looked all around the spring, and at last Ted found a place where it seemed as if some one had run through in a hurry, for twigs were broken off the bushes, and, by looking down at the ground, he saw the marks of shoes in the dirt.

Of course Ted could not tell who had made them, but he thought surely it must have been the tramp who had pulled Trouble from the spring. Ted was sure they were not the footprints of himself and his sister, for their own were much smaller.

"Come on, Jan!" cried Teddy. "We'll find that tramp now or, anyway, the place where he hides."

He pushed on through the bushes. There seemed to be a sort of path leading away from the spring, which was not the same path that Ted and Grandpa Martin took when they went from the camp to the waterhole to fill the pail each day.

On and on went Ted, with Jan following. She was so excited now at the thought that perhaps they might find something, that she was not a bit frightened.

"Wait a minute! Wait for me, Teddy!" she called, as her brother hurried on ahead of her.

"Come on, Jan!" he called. "There's a good path here, and I guess I see something. Oh, look here! Oh, Jan! Oh! Oh!" suddenly cried Teddy. Then his voice seemed to fade away, as if he had all at once gone down the cellar, and Jan could hear him calling faintly.

"Oh, Teddy! What's the matter? What's the matter?" she cried as she ran on through the bushes.

"I've found the cave!" was his answer, so faint and far away that Jan could hardly hear. "I've found the cave. I fell right into it! Come on!"

CHAPTER X

THE GRAPEVINE SWING

Wondering what had happened to her brother, Jan hurried on toward the place from which his voice came. It sounded more than ever as if he were down a cellar.

"But there can't be any cellars in these woods," thought the little girl.

"Where are you, Teddy?" she called after a bit. "I can't see you!"

"Here I am, right behind you!" was the answer, and Jan, turning quickly, saw the head of her brother sticking up out of a hole in the ground.

"Oh! Oh!" exclaimed Ted's sister. "Where's the rest of you? Where's your legs and your feet?"

"Down in the hole," explained Teddy. "I'm in the cave. I fell in. That's how I found it."

"Is it a real cave?" asked Janet.

"It is. It goes away back under the ground, only I didn't go in 'cause it's so dark. I'm going to get a light and see what's there."

"I'm not!" said Jan, very decidedly.

"Well, then I'll get grandpa. Maybe this is the cave where the tramps live. Come and look where I am. You won't fall in."

"How did you find it?" asked Janet, as she walked toward the hole, down in which Teddy was standing. It was a little way from the path the two Curlytops had walked along through the woods—the path leading from the spring.

"I just fell in it, I told you," Ted answered. "I was walking along, and, all at once, I slipped down through the dried leaves. First I thought I was going down in a big hole, but it isn't over my head and a lot of leaves went down with me, so I didn't get jounced hardly at all."

Jan went to the edge and looked down in the hole. It seemed to be a large one in between two big rocks, and Ted showed her where the hole slanted downward and went farther underground. It was dark there, and Jan made up her mind she would never go into it, even if Ted did.

The Grapevine Swing

"You'd better come up," she said at last. "Maybe mother wouldn't like it. Besides, there might be snakes down in there."

"Oh! I didn't think about them!" exclaimed Ted, and he tried to scramble up, but it was not so easy as he had hoped. He was a little excited, too, since Janet had spoken of snakes. Teddy did not like them, and they might be in among the leaves that had fallen down into the hole with him.

"Can't you get up?" Jan asked, when her brother had slipped back two or three times.

"Maybe I could if you'd let me take hold of your hand," suggested Teddy.

"Then you'd pull me in, and we'd both be down there."

Ted saw that this was so. He tried again to get out, but could not, for mixed with the leaves were many dry, brown pine needles from the trees growing overhead; and if you have ever been in the woods you know how slippery pine needles are when the ground is covered with them. Teddy slipped back again and again.

"Oh, Ted! can't you *ever* get up?" asked Janet, almost ready to cry.

"Oh, I'll get out somehow," he said. Then dangling down from a tree behind his sister, he saw a long wild grapevine, which was almost like a piece of rope.

"If I had hold of that I could pull myself out," Teddy said. "See if you can reach it to me, Jan."

After two or three trials his sister did this. Then, holding to a loose end of the grapevine while the other end was twined fast round a tree, Teddy pulled himself out of the hole. Once on firm ground he made the loose end of the grapevine fast to a stone that lay near the edge of the hole.

"What made you do that?" asked Janet.

"So the next time I get down there I can pull myself out," Teddy answered.

"Are you going down there again?" Jan queried.

"Course I am!" declared Ted. "I didn't half look in the cave. It's a big place. I could see in only a little way, 'cause it was so dark. I'm goin' to tell grandpa and have him bring a lantern."

Grandpa Martin was surprised when Ted and Jan told him what they had found in the woods.

"I didn't suppose there was a cave on the island," said the farmer. "I must have a look at it."

"And may I come? And will you take a lantern?" asked Teddy eagerly.

"Well, yes, I guess so," said grandpa slowly.

"Oh, Father, do you think it is safe?" asked Mrs. Martin.

"Yes, I think so. I won't go very far in with the children. It may be only the den of a fox or some small animal, and not a real cave."

"I think it's a big cave," declared Ted. "Come on, Grandpa."

"Me come!" cried Trouble, as the two Curlytops set off with Grandpa Martin through the woods, toward the place where Teddy had fallen down with the pile of leaves. "Me come!"

"No, you stay with me," laughed Mother Martin, catching him up in her arms. Trouble did not want to stay behind, not having been with his brother and sister of late as much as he wished. "We'll bake a patty-cake!" Mrs. Martin added, and then Trouble laughed, for he liked to help Nora bake. That is, he thought he helped. And at least he helped to eat what Nora took out of the oven.

"Now show me where the cave is," said

Grandpa Martin to Ted, as they neared the place. "But be careful not to fall into it again."

"Oh, I've got a grapevine rope so I can pull myself out," said Jan's brother. "Here it is, over this way."

Teddy Martin was an observing little fellow. He could find his way around in the woods very well, once he had been to a place, and he did not go wrong this time. He led his grandfather right to the entrance of the cave.

And it proved to be a real cave. Grandpa Martin found this out when he jumped down into the place where Teddy had fallen, and when the lantern had been lighted and flashed into the dark hole.

"Yes, it's a cave all right," the children's grandfather said. "And to think the many times I've been on this island I never found it! Well, I'll go in a little way."

"Can't I come?" asked Ted, as he saw his grandfather start into the dark hole which spread out from the open place into which Ted had fallen.

"I'm not coming," declared Janet, "and I don't want to stay here all alone."

"You stay there with your sister, Curlytop," directed Mr. Martin. "If I find out it's all right and is safe, I'll come back and take you both in a little way."

Grandpa Martin walked into the dark hole, his lantern flickering like a firefly at night. The Curlytops watched it until they could no longer see the gleam. Then they waited expectantly.

"Maybe somethin'll grab grandpa," said Jan, after a bit.

"What?" asked Ted.

"A fox—or somethin'!"

"Pooh, he isn't afraid of a fox!"

"Well, a bear, maybe!"

"There isn't any bears here, Janet Martin! I'm not afraid."

Perhaps Ted said this because, just then, he saw his grandfather coming out of the cave. The farmer had not been gone very long.

"Is it a cave?" called Ted.

"A sure-enough one?" added his sister.

"Yes, it's a sure-enough cave. But there's nothing in it."

"No wild animals?" Jan demanded.

"Not even a mouse, as far as I could see," laughed Mr. Martin. "But some one **had** been in the cave eating his lunch."

"Maybe there was a picnic, Grandpa," suggested Ted.

"No, I think only one or two persons were in the big hole," said his grandfather. "For it *is* a big hole, larger than I thought it was. I could stand up straight once I was inside."

"Take us in!" begged Ted.

"Yes, I think it will be all right. Come along, Jan. I'll hold your hand, and there isn't anything of which to be afraid. Come on!"

So Janet and Teddy went into the cave. By the light of grandpa's lantern they could see that it was a large place, a regular underground house—a cave just like those of which they had read in fairy stories.

"And was there somebody here, really?" asked Ted eagerly.

"Yes," answered his grandfather. "See. Here are bits of bread scattered about, and papers in which some one brought his lunch here."

"Maybe it was the tramps," whispered Janet.

"Maybe," agreed Mr. Martin. "I must have another look over the island."

There was not much else in the cave that they could see with the one lantern. Grandpa Martin wanted to look about more, and back in the far corners, but he did not like to take the children along, and Jan held tightly to his hand as if she feared she would lose him.

"I'll come here alone some other time, and see what I can find," thought Grandpa Martin to himself, as they came out.

"I don't like it in there," said Jan, once they were again out in the sunshine. "I don't like caves."

"I do," declared Ted. "When Hal Chester comes to visit me, as he said he would, he and I will look all through this cave."

"Is Hal coming?" asked Jan, remembering the boy, once lame but now cured, who had played with them and told them about Princess Blue Eyes.

"Yes, mother asked him to come and spend a week, and he said he would. We'll have some fun in the cave."

"What do you suppose the big hole can be?" asked Mrs. Martin, when Grandpa Martin and the children reached camp after their visit to the strange place.

"I don't know," he answered. "It doesn't seem to have been dug with picks and shovels. It's just a natural cave I guess, and some fishermen may have eaten their lunch there one day when it rained. But there is no one in it now."

Ted and Jan talked much about the cave the rest of that day. They went for a ride in the wagon drawn by Nicknack, taking Trouble with them. On their way back Jan said:

"Oh, I wish I had a swing."

"It would be fun," agreed Ted. "Maybe I can make one."

"You'll have to get a rope," said his sister. "Grandpa is going to row over in the boat to-morrow. Ask him to bring us one."

"No, he don't need to bring us a rope," went on her brother.

"Why not?"

" 'Cause I can get a rope in the woods."

"A rope in the woods? Oh, Teddy Martin, you can not! Ropes don't grow on trees."

"The kind I mean does," answered Ted with a laugh. "Wait and I'll show you."

When Nicknack had been put in the new stable which Grandpa Martin had built for him, Teddy, followed by Jan and Trouble, walked a little way into the woods. Ted carried with him a piece of old carpet.

The Grapevine Swing 121

"What's that for?" his sister asked.

"For a swing board," he answered.

"But where's the swing rope?"

"Here!" cried Ted suddenly. He pointed to a long wild grapevine, which hung dangling between two trees, around which it was twined. The vine was a very long one, and as thick around as the piece Teddy had used to pull himself out of the hole near the cave. It did seem like a regular swing.

"Well—maybe," murmured Jan.

"Now we can have some fun!" cried Ted. He folded the piece of carpet and laid it over the grapevine. Then he sat down, gave a push on the ground with his feet, and away he swung as nicely as though he was in a regular swing, made with a rope from the store.

"Oh, how nice!" cried Janet. "Let me try it, Teddy."

"Wait till I see if it's strong enough."

He swung back and forward several more times and then let his sister try it. She, too, swayed to and fro in the grapevine swing, which was in a shady place in the woods. Then Trouble, who had seen what was going on, cried:

"I want to swing, too! I want to swing!"

"I'll take you on my lap," offered Janet, and this she did.

"I'll push you," offered Teddy, and he gave his sister and his baby brother a long push in the grapevine swing.

But, just as they were going nicely and Trouble was laughing in delight, there was a sudden cracking sound and Janet cried:

"Oh, I'm falling! I'm falling! The swing is coming down!"

And that is just what happened.

CHAPTER XI

TROUBLE MAKES A CAKE

WITH a crackle and a snap the grapevine swing sagged down on one side. Janet tried to hold Trouble in her arms, but he slipped from her lap, just as she slipped off the piece of carpet which Ted had folded for the seat of the swing. Then Janet toppled down as the vine broke, and she and her little brother came together in a heap on the ground.

"Oh!" exclaimed Ted. "Are you hurt?"

Neither Jan nor Trouble answered him for a moment. Then Baby William began to cry. Jan lay still on the ground for a second or two, and then she jumped up with a laugh.

"I'm not hurt a bit!" she said. "I fell right in a pile of leaves, and it was like jouncing up and down in the hay."

"What's the matter with Trouble?" asked Ted.

Baby William kept on crying.

"Never mind!" put in Jan. "Sister'll kiss it and make it all better! Where is you hurt, Trouble dear?"

The little fellow stopped crying and looked up at Jan, his eyes filled with tears.

"My posy-tree is hurted," he said, holding a broken flower out to his sister. "Swing broked my posy-tree!"

Trouble called any weed, flower or bunch of grass he happened to pick a "posy-tree."

"Oh, I guess he isn't hurt," remarked Teddy. "If it's only a broken posy-tree I'll get you another," he said kindly. "Are you all right, Trouble? Can you stand up?" for he feared, after all, lest Baby William's legs might have been hurt, since they were doubled up under him.

Trouble showed he was all right by getting up and walking about. He had stopped crying, and Ted and Jan could see that he, too, had fallen on a pile of soft leaves near the swing, so he was only "jiggled up," as Jan called it.

One side of the grapevine swing had torn loose from the tree, and thus it had come down with Jan and Trouble.

"I guess it wasn't strong enough for two,"

Trouble Makes a Cake

said Ted. "Maybe I can find another grapevine."

"I'd like a rope swing better," Janet said. "Then it wouldn't tumble down."

"I guess that's so," agreed her brother. "We'll ask grandpa to get one."

Grandpa Martin laughed when he heard what had happened to the grapevine swing, and promised to make a real one of rope for the Curlytops. This he did a day or so afterward, so that Ted and Jan had a fine swing in their camp on Star Island, as well as one at Cherry Farm. They were two very fortunate children, I think, to have such a grandfather.

"Where are you going now, Grandpa?" called Jan one day, as she saw the farmer getting the boat ready for use.

"I'm going over to the mainland to get some things for our camp," answered Mr. Martin. "They came from a big store in some boxes and crates, and they're at the railroad station. I'm going over to get them. Do you Curlytops want to come along?"

"Well, I just guess we do!" cried Ted.

"Me want to come!" begged Trouble.

"Not this time, Dear," said his mother.

"You stay with me, and we will have some fun. Let Jan and Ted go."

Trouble was going to cry, but when Nora gave him a cookie he changed his mind and ate the little cake instead, though I think one or two tears splotched down on it and made it a bit salty. But Trouble did not seem to mind.

Ted and Jan had lots of fun riding back in the boat to the main shore with their grandfather. When the boat was almost at the dock Mr. Martin let the two children take hold of one of the oars and help him row. Of course the Curlytops could not pull very much, but they did pretty well, and it helped them to know how a boat is made to go through the water, when it has no steam engine or gasolene motor to make it glide along, or sails on which the wind can blow to push it.

"You can't know too much about boats and the water, especially when you are camping on an island in the middle of a lake," said Grandpa Martin. "When you get bigger, Ted and Jan, you'll be able to row a boat all by yourselves."

"Maybe day after to-morrow," suggested Jan.

"I wish I could now," said Ted.

Trouble Makes a Cake

"Oh, but you're too small!" his grandfather said.

The boat was tied to the wharf, and then, getting an expressman to go to the depot for the boxes and crates, Mr. Martin took the children with him on the wagon.

"We're having lots of fun!" cried Jan, as the horse trotted along. "We're camping and we had a ride in a boat and now we're having a ride in a wagon."

"Lots of fun!" agreed Ted. "I'm glad we've got grandpa!"

"And grandpa is glad he has you two Curlytops to go camping with him!" laughed the farmer, as the expressman made his horse go faster.

At the depot, while the children were waiting to have the boxes and crates of things for the camp loaded into the wagon, Ted saw Arthur Weldon, a boy with whom he sometimes played.

"Hello, Art!" called Ted.

"Hello!" answered Arthur. "I thought you were camping on Star Island."

"We are," answered Teddy.

"It doesn't look so!" laughed Arthur, or "Art," as most of his boy friends called him.

"Well, we just came over to get some things. There's grandpa and the expressman with them now," went on Ted, as the two men came from the freight house with a number of bundles.

"I wish I was camping," went on the other boy. "It isn't any fun around here."

"You can come over to see us sometimes," invited Jan. "I'll ask my mother to let you, and you can play with us."

"He don't want to play girls' games!" cried Ted.

"Well, I guess I can play boys' games as well as girls' games!" exclaimed Janet, with some indignation.

"Oh, yes, course you can," agreed her brother.

"And maybe Art can bring his sister to the island to see us, and then we could play boys' games and girls', too," went on Jan.

"I'll ask my mother," promised Arthur.

Grandpa and the expressman soon had the wagon loaded, and Arthur rode back in it with the Curlytops to the wharf where the boat was tied.

"All aboard for Star Island!" cried Mr. Martin, when the things were in the boat, nearly filling it. "All aboard!"

Trouble Makes a Cake 129

"I wish I could come now!" sighed Arthur.

"Well, we'd like to take you," said Grandpa Martin, "but it wouldn't be a good thing to take you unless your mother knew you were coming with us, and we haven't time to go up to ask her now. The next time maybe we'll take you back with us."

There was a wistful look on Arthur's face as he watched the boat being rowed away from the main shore and toward the island. Ted and Janet waved their hands to him, and said they would ask their mother to invite him for a visit, which they did a few weeks later.

Once back on the island the things were taken out of the boat and then began the work of taking them out of the boxes and crates. There was a new oil stove, to warm the tent on cool or rainy days, and other things for the camp, and when all had been unpacked there was quite a pile of boards and sticks left.

"I know what we can do with them," said Teddy to Janet, when they had been piled in a heap not far from the shore of the lake, and a little distance away from the tents.

"What?" asked the little girl.

"We can make a raft like Robinson Crusoe did," answered Teddy, for his mother had read him a little about the shipwrecked sailor who, as told in the story book, lived so long alone on an island.

"What's a raft?" asked Janet.

"Oh, it's something like a boat, but it hasn't got any sides to it—only a bottom," answered her brother. "You make it out of flat boards and you have to push it along with a pole. We can make a raft out of all the boards and pieces of wood grandpa took the things out of. It'll be a lot of fun!"

"Will mother let us?" asked Jan.

"Oh, I guess so," answered Teddy.

But he did not go to ask to find out. He found a hammer where grandpa had been using it to knock apart the crates and boxes, and, with the help of Jan, Teddy was soon making his raft. There were plenty of nails which had come out of the boxes and crates. Some of them were rather crooked, but when Ted tried to hammer them straight he pounded his fingers.

"That hurts," he said. "I guess crooked nails are as good as straight ones. Anyhow this raft is going to be crooked."

And it was very crooked and "wobboly,"

as Janet called it, when Teddy had shoved it into the water and, taking off his shoes and stockings, got on it.

"Come on, Jan!" he cried, "I'm going to have a ride."

"No, it's too tippy," Janet answered.

"Oh, it can't tip over," said Teddy. "That's what a raft is for—not to tip over. Maybe you can slide off, but it can't tip over. Come on!"

So Janet took off her shoes and stockings.

Now of course she ought not to have done that, nor ought Teddy to have got on the raft without asking his mother or his grandfather. But then the Curlytops were no different from other children.

So on the raft got Teddy and Janet, and for a time they had lots of fun pushing it around a shallow little cove, not far from the shore of Star Island. A clump of trees hid them from the sight of Mother Martin and grandpa at camp.

"Let's go farther out," suggested Teddy, after a bit.

"I'm afraid," replied Janet.

"Aw, it'll be all right!" cried Ted. "I won't let it tip over!"

So Janet let him pole out a little farther,

until she saw that the shore was far away, and then she cried:

"I want to go back!"

"All right," answered Ted. "I don't want anybody on my raft who's a skeered. I'll go alone!"

He poled back to shore and Janet got off the raft. Then Teddy shoved the wabbly mass of boards and sticks, fastened together with crooked nails, out into the lake again. He had not gone very far before something happened. One end of the raft tipped up and the other end dipped down, and—off slid Teddy into the water.

"Oh! Oh!" screamed Janet. "You'll be drowned! I'm going to tell grandpa."

She ran to the camp with the news, and Mr. and Mrs. Martin came hurrying back. By this time Teddy had managed to get up and was standing in the water, which was not deep.

"I—I'm all right," he stammered. "Only I—I'm—wet!"

"I should say you *were!*" exclaimed his mother. "You mustn't go on any more rafts."

Teddy promised that he would not, and then, when he had put on dry clothes, he and

Trouble Makes a Cake 133

Janet played other games that were not so dangerous. They had lots of fun in the camp on Star Island.

"Come on, Jan!" called her brother one morning after breakfast. "Come on down to the lake."

"What're you goin' to do?" she asked.

"I think he had better look for the 'g' you dropped," said Mrs. Martin with a laugh.

"What 'g?' " asked Jan.

"The one off 'going,' " was the answer. "You must be more careful of your words, Janet dear. Learn to talk nicely, and don't drop your 'g' letters."

She had been trying to teach this to the Curlytops for a long while, and they were almost cured of leaving off the final "g" of their words. But, once in a while, just as Jan did that time, they forgot.

"What are you going to do?" asked Janet, slowly and carefully this time.

"Sail my boat," answered Ted. "I'll give your doll a ride if you want me to."

"Not this one," replied his sister, looking at the one she carried. It had on a fine red dress.

"Why not that doll?" Ted inquired.

" 'Cause your boat might tip over and

spill my doll in the lake. Then she'd be spoiled and so would her dress. Wait. I'll get my rubber doll. Water won't hurt her."

"My boat won't tip over," Ted declared. "It's a good one."

But even Jan's rubber doll must have been too heavy for Ted's small boat, for, half way across a little shallow cove in the lake, where the Curlytops waded and Ted sailed his ships, the boat tipped to one side, and the doll was thrown into the water.

"There! I told you so!" cried Janet.

"Well, she's rubber, and you can pretend she has on a bathing suit an' has gone in swimming!" declared Ted.

"But maybe a fish'll bite a hole in her and then she can't whistle through the hole in her back!" wailed Jan, ready to cry.

"There's no fish here, only baby ones; and they can't bite," Ted answered. "But I'll get her for you, Jan."

He waded out, set his ship upright again, and brought his sister's doll to shore. Nancy—which was the doll's name—did not seem to have been hurt by falling into the lake. Her painted smile was the same as ever.

"I guess I'll dress her now so she won't

Trouble Makes a Cake 135

get cold after her bath," said Jan, who sometimes acted as though her dolls were really alive. She liked her playthings very much indeed.

While his sister went back to the tent with her doll Ted sailed his boat. Then Trouble came down to the edge of the little cove, and began to take off his shoes and stockings to go wading as Ted was doing. Ted was not sure whether or not his mother wanted Baby William to do this, so he decided to run up to the camp to ask.

"Don't go in the water until I come back, Trouble," Ted ordered his little brother.

But the sight of the cool, sparkling water was too much for Baby William.

Off came his shoes and stockings without waiting for Ted to come back to say whether or not Mother Martin would let him go splashing in the water. Into the lake Baby William went. And he was not careful about getting wet, either, so that when Ted came back with his mother, who wanted to make sure that her baby boy was all right, they saw him out in the middle of the cove with Ted's boat. And the water was half way up to Trouble's waist, the lower part of his bloomers being soaked.

"Oh, you dear bunch of Trouble!" cried his mother. "You mustn't do that!"

"Havin' fun!" was all Trouble said.

"Come here!" cried Mrs. Martin.

"Wait till I sail boat," and he pushed Ted's toy about in the cove, splashing more water on himself.

"I guess you'll have to get him," said Mrs. Martin to Teddy, who half dragged, half led his little brother to shore. Trouble got wetter than ever during this, and his mother had to take him back to the tent to put dry things on him.

"Trouble," she said, "you are a bad little boy. I'll have to keep you in camp the rest of the day now. After this you must not go in wading until I say you may. If you had had your bathing suit on it would have been all right. Now you must be punished."

Trouble cried and struggled, but it was of no use. When Mother Martin said a thing must be done it was done, and Trouble could not play in the water again that day.

Toward the middle of the afternoon, however, as he had been pretty good playing around the tent, he was allowed to roam farther off, though told he must not go near the water.

Trouble Makes a Cake

"You stay with me, Baby," called Nora. "I'm going to bake a cake and I'll give you some."

"Trouble bake a cake, too?" he asked.

"No, Trouble isn't big enough to bake a cake, but you can watch me. I'll get out the flour and sugar and other things, and I'll make a little cake just for you."

On a table in the cooking tent Nora set out the things she was to use for her baking. There was the bag of flour, some water in a dish and other things. Just as she was about to mix the cake Mrs. Martin called Nora away for a moment.

"Now, Trouble, don't touch anything until I come back!" warned the girl, as she hurried out of the tent. "I won't be gone a minute."

But she was gone longer than that. Left alone in the tent, with many things on the table in front of him, Trouble looked at them. He knew he could have lots of fun with some of the pans, cups, the egg beater, the flour, the water and the eggs. A little smile spread over his tanned, chubby face.

"Trouble bake a cake," he said to himself. "Nora bake a cake—Trouble bake a cake. Yes!"

First Baby William pulled toward him the bag of flour. He managed to do it without upsetting it, for the bag was a small one. Near it was a bowl of water with a spoon in it. Trouble had seen his mother and Nora bake cakes, and he must have remembered that they mixed the flour and water together. Anyhow that was the way to make mud pies —by mixing sand and water.

Trouble looked for something to mix his cake in. The tins and dishes were so far back on the table that he could not get them easily. He must take something else.

Off his head Trouble pulled his white hat —a new one that grandpa had brought only that day from the village store.

"Make cake in dis," murmured Baby William to himself.

He pushed a chair up to the table and climbed upon it. From the chair he got on the table and sat down. Then he began to make his cake in his hat.

CHAPTER XII

THE CURLYTOPS GO SWIMMING

"Trouble make a cake—Trouble make a nice cake for Jan an' Ted," murmured Baby William to himself. Certainly he thought he was going to do that—make a nice cake—but it did not turn out just that way.

Trouble's hat, being of felt, held water just as a dish or a basin would have done, but the little fellow had to hold it very carefully in his lap between his knees as he sat on the table, or he would have squeezed his hat and the water would have spilled out. But when Trouble really wanted to do anything he could be very careful. And he wanted, very much this time, to make that cake.

So, when he had the water in his hat he began to dip up some flour from the bag with a large spoon.

When the little fellow thought he had

enough flour sifted into the water in his hat he began to stir it, just as he had seen Nora stir her cake batter. Around and around he stirred it, and then he found that his cake was much too wet. He had not enough flour in it, just as, sometimes, when he and Jan made mud pies, they did not have enough sand or dirt in the water to make the stuff for the pies as thick as they wanted it.

So Trouble stirred in more flour. And then, just as you can easily guess, he made it too thick, and had to put in more water.

By this time Trouble's small hat was almost full of flour and water, and some dough began to run over the edges, down on his little bare legs, and also on his rompers and on the table and even to the floor of the kitchen tent.

Trouble did not like that. He wanted to get his cake mixed before Nora came back, so she could bake it in the oven for him. For he knew cakes must be baked to make them good to eat, and he really hoped, knowing no better, that his cake would be good enough to eat.

"Trouble make a big cake," he said, as he slowly put a little more water into his hat, and stirred the dough some more. He

THEN TROUBLE BEGAN TO MAKE A CAKE IN HIS HAT.

The Curlytops on Star Island Page 138

splashed some of the flour and water on the end of his stubby nose, and wiped it off on the back of his hand. Then, as he kept on stirring, some more of the dough splashed on his cheeks, and he had to wipe that off. So that, by this time, Baby William had on his hands and face at least as much dough as there was in the spoon.

But finally the little mischief-maker got the dough in his hat just about thick enough —not too much flour and not too much water in it. When this point was reached he knew that it was time to get ready for the baking part—putting the dough in the pans so it would go into the oven.

Trouble wanted to do as much toward making his own cake as he could without asking Nora to help. So now he thought he could put the dough in the baking pans himself. But they were on the table beyond his reach. He must get up to reach them.

So Trouble got up, and then——

Well, you can just imagine what happened. He forgot that he was holding in his lap the hat full of dough and as soon as he stood up of course that slipped from his lap and the table and went splashing all over the floor.

"Squee-squish-squash!" the hat full of dough dropped.

"Oh!" exclaimed Trouble. "Oh!"

His feet were covered with the white flour and water. Some splashed on Nora's chair near the table, some splashed on the table legs and more spread over the tent floor and ran in little streams toward the far edges. And, in the midst of it, like a little island in the middle of a lake of dough, was Trouble's new hat. Only now you could hardly tell which was the hat and which was the dough.

"Trouble's cake all gone!" said the little fellow sadly, and just as he said that back came Nora. She gave one look inside her nice, clean tent-kitchen—at least it had been clean when she left it—and then she cried:

"Oh, Trouble Martin! What *have* you gone and done?"

"Trouble make a cake but it spill," he said slowly, climbing down from the table.

"Spill! I should say it did spill!" cried Nora. "Oh, what a sight you are! And what will your mother say!"

"What is it now, Nora?" asked Mrs. Martin, who heard the noise in the kitchen.

"Oh, it's Trouble, as you might guess.

The Curlytops Go Swimming 143

He's tried to make a cake. But—such a mess!"

Mrs. Martin looked in. She wanted to laugh and cry at the same time, but, as that is rather hard to do, she did neither. She just stood and looked at Trouble. He had picked up his hat, which still had a little of the paste in it, and this was now dripping down the front of his rompers.

"Well, it's clean dirt, not like the time he was stuck in the mud of the brook at home, that's one consolation," said Nora at last. Nora had a good habit of trying to make the best of everything.

"Yes, it's clean dirt and it will wash off," agreed Mother Martin. "But, oh, Trouble! You are *such* a sight! And so is Nora's kitchen."

"Oh, well, I don't mind cleaning up," said the good-natured maid. "Come on, Trouble, I'll let your mother wash you and then I'll finish the cake."

"Make a cake for Trouble?" asked Baby William.

"Yes, I guess I'll have to, since you couldn't make one for yourself," laughed Nora. "Never mind, you'll be a man when you grow up and you won't have to mess around a kitchen. Here you are!" and she caught him up, all doughy as he was, and carried him to the big tent where his mother soon had him washed and in clean clothes.

Then Nora cleaned up the kitchen and made some real cakes and cookies which Ted and Jan, as well as Trouble, ate a little later. The Curlytops laughed when told of Trouble's attempt to make a cake, and for a long time after that whenever they were telling any of their friends about the queer things their baby brother did, they always told first about the cake he made in his hat one day.

"Oh, Ted, I know what let's do!" cried Janet one day, about a week after Trouble had played with the flour and water.

"What?" asked her brother. "Go fishing?"

"No, I don't like fishing. Anyhow we went fishing once, and I don't like to see the worms wiggle. Let's make a little play tent for ourselves in the woods."

"We haven't any cloth."

"We can make one of leaves and branches, just like the bower we made for Nicknack before grandpa put up the little board barn for him."

"Yes, we can do that," agreed Ted. "It'll be fun. Come on."

A little later the two Curlytops were cutting down branches from low trees, sticking the ends into the soft ground, and tying the leafy tops together with string. This made a sort of tent, and though there were holes in it, where the leaves did not quite come together, it made a shady place.

Jan brought in her dolls, and Ted his sailboat and other toys, and there the two children played for some little time. Trouble was not with them.

"But he'll be along pretty soon," remarked Janet, "and he'll want part of the tent for his. Is it big enough for three, Teddy?"

"Well, we can make Trouble a little bower for himself right next door. He'll want to bring in a lot of old stones and mud pies anyhow, and we don't want them. We'll make a little bower for him when he comes along."

So, waiting for their little brother to hunt them out, which he always did sooner or later if they went off to play without him, Ted and Jan had fun in the little leafy house they had made for themselves.

They were having a good time, and were wondering if Grandpa Martin would ever find the queer ragged man or if they would see the strange blue light again, when Jan suddenly gave a scream.

"What's the matter?" asked Ted.

"Something tickled the back of my neck," explained his sister. "Maybe it's a big worm, or a caterpillar! Look, Ted, will you?"

Teddy turned to look, but, as he did so, he gave a cry of surprise.

"It's a goat! It's our goat! It's Nicknack!" yelled Teddy. "He's stuck his head right through the bower and, oh, Jan! he's eating it!"

And so Nicknack was. His head was halfway through the side of the tree-tent nearest Jan and the goat was chewing some of the green leaves. It was Nicknack's whiskers that had tickled Jan on the back of her neck.

"Whoa there, Nicknack!" called Ted, as the goat from the outside pushed his way farther into the tent. "Whoa, there! You'll upset this place in a minute!"

And so it seemed Nicknack would do, for he was hungrily eating the leaves of the

The Curlytops Go Swimming 147

branches from which Jan and Ted had made their playhouse.

"How'd he get loose?" asked Jan.

"I don't know," Ted answered. "I tied him good and tight by his rope. I wonder if——"

Just then a voice called:

"Wait for me, Nicknack! Wait for me!"

"It's Trouble!" cried Jan and Ted together.

Ted looked out through the hole the goat had eaten in the side of the bower, and saw Baby William toddling toward him.

"Did you let Nicknack loose?" demanded Ted.

"Ess, I did," answered Trouble. "I cutted his wope with a knife, I did. I wants a wide. Wait for me, Nicknack!"

The goat was in no hurry to get away, for he liked to eat the green leaves, and Ted, coming out of the bower, which was almost ready to fall down now that the goat was half-way inside it, saw where the rope, fast around his pet's horns, had been cut.

"You mustn't do that, Trouble," Ted said to his little brother. "You mustn't cut Nicknack's rope. He might run away into the lake."

"Trouble wants a wide."

"Well, we'll give you a ride," added Jan. "But did mother or Nora give you the knife to cut the rope?"

"No. Trouble got knife offen table."

"Oh, you must *never* do that!" cried Jan. "You might fall on the sharp knife and cut yourself. Trouble was bad!"

The little fellow had really taken a knife from the table, and had sawed away with it on Nicknack's rope until he had cut it through. Then Nicknack had wandered over to the green bower to get something to eat, and Trouble, dropping the knife, had followed.

Mrs. Martin, to punish Baby William so he would remember not to take knives again, would not let him have a goat ride, and he cried very hard when Ted and Jan went off without him. But even little boys must learn not to do what is wrong, and Trouble was no different from any others.

One afternoon, when the Curlytops had been wandering around the woods of the island, looking to see if any berries were yet ripe, they came back to camp rather tired and warm.

"I know what would be nice for you," said

Nora, who came to the flap doorway of the kitchen tent. "Yes, I know *two* things that would be nice for you."

"What?" asked Jan, fanning herself with her sunbonnet.

"I hope it's something good to eat," sighed Teddy, as he sat down in the shade.

"Part of it," answered Nora. "How would you like some cool lemonade—that is, when you are not so warm," she added quickly, for Teddy had jumped up on hearing this, and was about to make a rush for the kind cook. "You must always rest a bit, when you are so warm from running, walking or playing, before you take a cold drink of anything."

"But have you any lemonade?" asked Janet, for she, too, was tired and thirsty.

"I'll make some, and you may have it when you are not so heated," went on the cook. "And I'll get some sweet crackers for you."

"That's nice," said Janet. "Are they the two things you were going to tell us to do, Nora?"

"No, I'll count the lemonade and crackers as one," went on the cook with a smile. "The other thing I was going to tell you to do is to take Nicknack and have a ride. That will cool you off if you go in the shade."

"Oh, so it will!" cried Ted. "We'll do it! And can we take the lemonade in a bottle, and the crackers in a bag, and put them in the goat-wagon?"

"Do you mean to give the crackers and lemonade a ride, too?" asked Mother Martin, who came out of her tent just then.

"No, but we can take them with us, and have a little picnic in the woods," explained Teddy. "We didn't find any berries, and so we didn't have any picnic."

"All right, Nora, give them the lemonade and crackers to take with them," said Mrs. Martin, smiling at the Curlytops.

"I'll go and make the cool drink now," said the cook.

"And I'll get the crackers," said the children's mother.

"And we'll go and get Nicknack and harness him to the cart," added Ted.

He and Janet were soon on their way to the little leafy bower where the goat was kept, for it was so warm on Star Island that the goat did not stay more than half the time in the stable Grandpa Martin had made for him.

The Curlytops Go Swimming 151

"Here, Nicknack! where are you?" called Teddy, as he neared the bower.

"Here, Nicknack!" called Janet.

But the goat did not answer. Nearly always, when he was called to in that way, he did, giving a loud "Baa-a-a-a-a!" that could be heard a long way.

"Oh, Nicknack isn't here!" cried Jan, when she saw the empty place. "Maybe he's run away, Ted."

"He must be on the island somewhere," said the little boy. "He can't row a boat and get off, and he doesn't like to swim, I guess, though he did fall into the water once."

"But where is he?" asked Janet.

"We'll look," Teddy said.

So the children peered about in the bushes, but not a sign of Nicknack could they see. They called and called, but the goat did not bleat back to them.

"Oh, where can he be?" asked Janet, and her eyes filled with tears, for she loved the pet animal very much.

"We'll look," said Teddy. "And if we can't find him we'll ask grandpa to help us look."

They wandered about, but not going too

far from the leafy bower, and, all at once, Ted cried:

"Hark! I hear him!"

"So do I!" added Janet. "Oh, where is he?"

"Listen!" returned her brother.

They both listened, hardly breathing, so as to make as little noise as possible. Once more they heard the cry of the goat:

"Baa-a-a-a-a-a!" went Nicknack. "Baa-a-a-a!"

"He's over this way!" cried Teddy, and he started to run to the left.

"No, I think he's here," and Janet pointed to the right.

"What's the matter, Curlytops?" asked Mrs. Martin, who came out just then to see what was keeping the children.

"We can hear Nicknack, but we can't see him," answered Ted.

Mrs. Martin listened to the goat's call.

"I think he's down this path," she said, and she took one midway between those Ted and Janet would have taken. "Come along!" she called back to the two children. "We'll soon find Nicknack."

"Here, Nicknack! Here, Nicknack!" called Ted.

"Come on, we want you to give us a ride!" added Janet.

But though the goat answered, as he nearly always did, his voice sounded afar off, and he did not come running to see his little friends.

"Oh, I wonder if anything is the matter with him?" asked Ted.

"We'll soon see," said Mrs. Martin.

Just then the barking of a dog was heard.

"Oh, I wonder if that's Skyrocket?" asked Janet.

"No, we left our dog home," said Mrs. Martin. "That sounds like a strange dog, and he seems to be barking at Nicknack. Come on, children. We'll see what the matter is!"

They hurried on, and, in a little while, they saw what had happened. Nicknack was caught in a thick bush by the rope around his horns. He had pulled the rope loose from his leafy bower, and it had dragged along after him as he wandered away. Then the end of the rope had become tangled in a thick bush and the goat could not pull it loose. He was held as tightly as if tied.

In front of him, but far enough away so the goat could not butt him with his horns, which Nicknack tried to do, was a big, and not very nice-looking, dog. This dog was barking fiercely at Nicknack, and the goat could not make him go away.

"Oh, Mother! don't let the dog hurt our goat!" begged Janet.

"I'll drive him away," cried Ted, catching up a stone.

"No, you had better let me do it," said Mrs. Martin. She picked up a stick and walked toward the dog, but he did not wait for her to get very close. With a last howl and a bark at Nicknack, the dog ran away, jumped into the lake and swam off toward shore. Then the rope was loosed and Nicknack, who was badly frightened, was led back by Ted and Jan and hitched to the wagon. He then gave them a fine ride. The dog was a stray one, which had swum over from the mainland, Grandpa Martin said.

Ted and Janet took the lemonade and crackers with them in the goat-wagon and had a nice little picnic in the woods.

"What can we do to-day?" asked Janet, as she and Teddy finished breakfast in the tent one morning, and, after playing about on the beach of the lake, wanted some other fun.

"Let's go swimming!" cried Teddy.

"And take Trouble with us," added his sister.

In their bathing suits and with Nora on the bank to watch them, the children were soon splashing in the cool water. Ted could swim a little bit, and Jan was just learning.

"Come on out where it's a little deeper," Ted urged his sister. "It isn't up to your knees here, and you can't swim in such shallow water."

"I'm afraid to go out," she said.

"Afraid of what?"

"Big fish or a crab."

"Pooh! those little crabs won't bite you, and when we splash around we scare away all the fish. They wouldn't bite you anyhow."

"Maybe a water snake would."

"No, it wouldn't," declared Ted. "Come on and see me swim."

So Jan waded out a little way with him. Ted was just taking a few strokes, really swimming quite well for so small a boy, when, all at once, he heard a cry from his sister.

"Oh, Ted! Ted!" she called. "Come on in, quick. A big fish is goin' to bite you!"

Ted gave one look over his shoulder and saw something with a pointed nose, long whiskers and two bright eyes swimming toward him.

"Oh!" yelled Ted, and he began running for shore as fast as he could splash through the water.

CHAPTER XIII

JAN'S QUEER RIDE

"What's the matter? What is it?" cried Nora from the bank where she was tossing bits of wood into the lake for Trouble to pretend they were little boats. "Have you got a cramp, Teddy boy?"

"It's a—a big fish—or—somethin'," he panted, as he kept on running and splashing the water all about, which, after all, did not matter as he was in his bathing suit.

"It's a shark after him!" cried Jan, who, by this time, was safe on shore, stopping on her way to grasp Trouble by the hand and lead him also to safety. "It's a shark!"

She had heard her mother read of bathers in the ocean being sometimes frightened by sharks, or by big fish that looked like sharks.

"Oh, a shark! Good land! We mustn't bathe here any more!" cried Nora.

By this time Ted was in such shallow

water that it was not much above his ankles. He could see the bottom, and he hoped no very big fish could swim in so little water. So he thought it would be safe to stop and look back.

"Oh, it's coming some more!" cried Jan, from where she stood on the bank with Nora and Trouble. "Look, Ted! It's coming."

The animal, fish, or whatever it was, indeed seemed to be coming straight for the shore near the place where the Curlytops were playing. Ted, Jan and Nora could see the sharp nose and the bright eyes more plainly now. As for Trouble, he did not know what it was all about, and he wanted to go back in the water to wade, which was as near swimming as he ever came.

Then the strange creature turned and suddenly made for a small rock, which stood out of the water a little way from the sandy beach. It climbed out on the rock, while the children and Nora watched eagerly, and then Ted gave a laugh.

"Why!" he exclaimed, "it's nothing but a big muskrat!"

"A muskrat?" echoed Jan.

"Yes."

"And see, he has a mussel, or fresh-water

clam," said Nora. "Look at him crack the shell."

And this is what the muskrat was really doing. It had been swimming in the lake— for muskrats are good swimmers—when it had found a fresh-water mussel, which is like a clam except that it has a longer shell that is black instead of white. Muskrats like mussels, but they cannot eat them in water.

They have to bring them up on shore, or to a flat rock or stump that sticks up out of water, where they can crack the shell and eat the mussel inside.

"If I'd a known what it was I wouldn't 'a' been scared," said Ted, who felt a little ashamed of himself for hurrying toward shore. "You frightened me yelling so, Jan."

"Well, I didn't want to see you get bit by a shark, Teddy. First I thought it was a shark."

"Well, sharks live in the ocean, where the water is salty," declared Ted.

"Anyhow maybe a muskrat bites," went on Janet.

"Well, maybe," agreed Ted. "I guess it's a good thing I didn't stay there when he came swimming in," for the big rat passed right over the place where Ted had been about to swim. "I'm glad you yelled, Janet."

"So'm I. I'm not going in swimming here any more."

"Oh, he won't come back," Ted said. "Come on!"

But Janet would not go, and as it was no fun for Ted to splash in the water all alone he stayed near shore and went wading with Trouble and his sister.

This was fun, and the Curlytops had a good time, while Nora, now that she knew there was no danger from sharks, sat in the shade and mended holes in the children's stockings.

"I wish we had a boat," said Ted after a while.

"Why, we have," answered Jan.

"Yes, I know, the big rowboat. But that's too heavy for me and you—I mean you and me," and Ted quickly corrected himself, for he knew it was polite always to name oneself last. "But I want a little boat that we can paddle around in."

Jan thought for a moment and then cried:

"Oh, I know the very thing!"

"What?" asked Ted eagerly.

"One of the boxes grandpa brought the things in from the store. They're long, and we can make box-boats of them. There's two of 'em!"

"That's what we can!" cried Teddy, as he thought of the boxes his sister meant. Groceries from the store had been sent to the camp in them. The boxes were strong, and long; big enough for Jan or Ted to sit down in them and reach over the sides to paddle, not being too high.

Mother Martin said they might take the boxes and make of them the play-boats they wanted, and, in great delight, Ted and his sister ran to get their new playthings.

Grandpa Martin pulled out all the nails that might scratch the children, and he also fastened strips of wood over the largest cracks in the boxes.

"That will keep out some of the water, but not all," he said. "Your box-boats won't float very long. They'll sink as soon as enough water runs in through the other cracks."

"Oh, well, we'll paddle in them in shallow water," promised Ted. "And sinking won't hurt, 'cause we've got on our bathing suits. Come on, Jan!"

Trouble wanted to sail in the new boats, also, but they were not large enough for two. Besides Mrs. Martin did not want the baby to be in the water too much. So she carried him away, Trouble crying and screaming to be allowed to stay, while Jan and Ted got ready for their first trip. They pretended the boats were ocean steamers and that the cove in the lake, near grandpa's camp, was the big ocean.

They had pieces of wood which their grandfather had whittled out for them to use as paddles, and, as Ted said, they could sit down in the bottoms of the box-boats and never mind how much water came in, for they still had on their bathing suits.

"All aboard!" called Teddy, as he got into his boat.

"I'm coming," answered Janet, pushing off from shore.

"Oh, I can really paddle!" cried Ted in delight, as he found that his box floated with him in it and he could send it along by using the board for a paddle, as one does in a canoe. "Isn't this great, Janet?"

"Oh, it's lots of fun!"

"I'm glad you thought of it. I never would," went on Ted. He was a good brother, for, whenever his sister did anything unusual like this he always gave her credit for it.

Around and around in the little cove paddled the Curlytops, having fun in their box-boats.

"I'm going to let the wind blow me," said Jan, after a bit. "I'm tired of paddling."

"There isn't any wind," Ted remarked.

"Well, what makes me go along, then?" asked his sister. "Look, I'm moving and I'm not paddling at all!"

She surely was. In her boat she was sailing right across the little cove, and, as Ted had said, there was not enough wind to blow a feather, to say nothing of a heavy box with a little girl in it.

"Isn't it queer!" exclaimed Janet. "What makes me go this way, Ted? You aren't sailing."

Ted's boat was not moving now, for he had stopped paddling.

Still Jan's craft moved on slowly but surely through the water. Then Ted saw a funny thing and gave a cry of surprise.

CHAPTER XIV

DIGGING FOR GOLD

"What's the matter?" called Jan. Her boat was now quite a little distance away from her brother's. "Do you see anything, Teddy?"

"I see you are being towed, Janet."

"Being what?"

"Towed—pulled along, you know, just like the mules pull the canal boats."

Once the Curlytops had visited a cousin who lived in the country near a canal, and they had seen the mules and horses walking along the canal towpath pulling the big boats by a long rope.

"Who's towing me, Ted?" asked Jan, trying to look over the side of her box. But, as she did so it tipped to one side and she was afraid it would upset, so she quickly sat down again.

"I don't know what it is," her brother

Digging for Gold

answered. "But something has hold of the rope that's fast to the front part of your box, and it's as tight as anything—the rope is. Something in the water is pulling you along."

On each of the box-boats the Curlytops had fastened a piece of clothesline their mother had given them. This line was to tie fast their boats to an overhanging tree branch, near the shore of the cove, when they were done playing.

And, as Ted had said, the rope fast to the end of Jan's box was stretched out tightly in front, the end being down under water.

"Oh, maybe it's the big muskrat that has hold of my rope and is giving me a ride," cried Janet. "It's fun!"

"No, I don't guess it's a rat," answered Teddy. "A muskrat wouldn't do that. Oh, I see what it is!" he cried suddenly. "I see it!"

"What?" asked Janet.

Again she got up and tried to look over the side of the box, but once more it tipped as though going to turn over and she sat down.

By this time both her box and Ted's was half full of water, and so went only very slowly along the little cove. The weight of the water that had leaked in through the cracks and the weight of the Curlytops themselves made the boxes float low in the lake.

"Can you see what's pulling me?" asked Janet.

"Yes," answered Teddy, "I can. It's a great big mud turtle!"

"A mud turtle!" cried Janet.

"I guess he's scared, too," said her brother, "for he's swimmin' all around as fast as anything!"

"Where is he?" asked Janet.

"Right in front of your boat. I guess your rope got caught around one of his legs, or on his shell, and he can't get it loose. He must have been swimming along and run into the rope. Or maybe he's got it in his mouth."

"If he had he could let go," answered Janet. "Oh, I see him!" she cried. She had stood up in her box and was looking over the front. The box had now sunk so low in the water that it was on the bottom of the little cove and no longer was the turtle towing it along.

The turtle, finding that it could no longer

swim, had come to the top of the water and was splashing about, trying to get loose. Jan could see it plainly now, as Ted had seen it before from his boat, which was still floating along, as not so much water had leaked in as had seeped into his sister's.

"Oh, isn't it a big one!" cried Jan. "It's a big turtle."

"It surely is!" assented Ted. "He could bite hard if he got hold of you."

"Is he biting my rope?" Janet asked.

"No, it's round one of his front legs," replied Ted. "There! he's got it loose!"

"There he goes!" shrieked Jan.

By this time the mud turtle, which was a very large one, had struggled and squirmed about so hard in the water that he had shaken loose the knot in the end of Jan's rope. The knot had been caught under its left front leg and when the turtle swam or crawled along on the bottom, the rope had been held tightly in place, and so the box was pulled along.

But when Jan's boat sank and went aground, the turtle could not pull it any farther, and had to back up, just as Nicknack the goat sometimes backed up his cart. This made the rope slack, or loose, and then the creature could shake the knot of the rope out from under its leg.

"There it goes!" cried Ted, as the turtle swam away. "Oh, what a whopper! It's bigger than the big muskrat!"

"Your muskrat didn't give you a ride Ted, and my turtle gave me a fine one," said Jan. "But I can't sail my boat any more."

"Well, we'll have to empty out some of the water. Then it will float again and you can get in it."

"I'm not going to let the rope drag in the water any more," decided Janet, after Ted had helped her tip her box over so the water would run out. "I don't really want any more rides like that. The next turtle might go out into the lake. I want to paddle."

"I wish a big whale would come along and tow me," laughed Ted. "I wouldn't let him go loose."

"He *might* pull you all across the lake," Janet said.

"I'd like that. Come on, we'll have a race."

"All right, Ted."

The Curlytops began paddling their box-boats about the cove once more. Ted won the race, being older and stronger than Janet, but she did very well.

Then after some more fun sailing about in their floating boxes the children were called by their mother, who said they had been in the water long enough. Besides dinner was ready, and they were hungry for the good things Nora had made.

"And didn't you find any of them, Father?" asked Mrs. Martin as the farmer pushed back his chair, when the meal was over.

"No, I didn't see a sign of them, and I looked all over the cave, too, Some persons have been sleeping in there, for I found a pile of old bags they had used for a bed, but I didn't find anyone."

"Find who?" Ted inquired.

"The tramps, or the ragged man you and Jan saw," answered his grandfather. "I have been looking about the island, but I could not find any of the ragged men, for I think there was more than one. So I guess they've gone, and we needn't think anything more about them."

"Did you see the blue light?" asked Ted.

"No, I didn't see that, either. I guess it wouldn't show in the daytime. But don't worry. Just have all the fun you can in camp. We can't stay here very much longer."

"Oh, do we have to go home?" cried the Curlytops, sorrowfully.

"Well, we can't stay here much longer," said Mother Martin. "In another month the weather will be too cold for living in a tent. Besides daddy will want us back, and grandpa has to gather in his farm crops for the winter. So have fun while you can."

"Isn't daddy coming here?" asked Jan.

"Yes, he'll be here next week to stay several days with us. Then he has to go back to the store."

The Curlytops had great fun when Daddy Martin came. They showed him all over the island—the cave, the place where Nicknack nearly ate up the bower-tent, the place where Ted saw the muskrat, and they even wanted him to go riding in the box-boats.

"Oh, I'm afraid I'm too big!" laughed Daddy Martin. "Besides, I'd be afraid if a mud turtle pulled me along."

"Oh, Daddy Martin! you would not!" laughed Janet.

And so the happy days went by, until Mr. Martin had to leave Star Island to go back

Digging for Gold 171

to his business. He promised to pay another visit, though, before the camp was ended.

Several times, before and after Daddy Martin's visit, Ted and Jan talked about the queer ragged man they had seen, and about the blue light and the cave.

"I wonder if we'll ever find out what it all means," said Jan. "It's like a story-book, isn't it, Ted?"

"A little, yes. But grandpa says not to be scared so I'm not."

"I'm not, either. But what do you s'pose that ragged man is looking for, and who is the professor?"

Teddy did not know, and said so. Then, when he and Jan got back to the tent, having been out with Trouble for a ride in the goat-cart, they found good news awaiting them.

"Here is a letter from Hal Chester, the little boy who used to be lame," said Mrs. Martin, for grandpa had come in, bringing the mail from the mainland post-office.

"Oh, can he come to pay us a visit?" asked Ted. His mother had allowed him to invite Hal.

"Yes, that's what he is going to do," went on Mrs. Martin. "His doctor says he is much better, and can walk with hardly a limp now, and the trip here will do him good. So to-morrow Grandpa Martin is going to bring him to Star Island."

"Oh, goody!" cried Ted and Jan, jumping up and down and clapping their hands. Trouble did the same thing, though he did not know exactly what for.

"We'll have fun with Hal!" cried Ted. "Maybe he'll help us find the tramp-man. Hal's smart—he can make kites and lots of things."

The next day Hal Chester came to visit the camp on Star Island.

"Say, this is a dandy place!" he exclaimed as he looked about at the tents and at the boat floating in the little cove. "I'll just love it here!"

"It's awful nice," agreed Jan.

"And there's a mystery here, too," added Ted.

"What do you mean?" Hal demanded. "What's a mystery?"

"Oh, it's something queer," went on Ted. "Something you can't tell what it is. This mystery is a tramp."

"A tramp?"

"Yes. Jan saw him when she was picking flowers, and he pulled Trouble out of the

Digging for Gold 173

spring afterward. And there's a cave here
where maybe he sleeps, 'cause there's some
bags for beds in it. He's looking for something on this island, that tramp-man is," declared Ted.

"Looking for something?" repeated Hal,
quite puzzled.

"Yes. He goes all around, and we saw
him picking up some stones. Didn't we,
Jan?"

"Yes, we did."

"Picking up stones," repeated Hal
slowly. Then he sprang up from where he
was sitting under a tree with the Curlytop
children.

"I know what he's looking for!" Hal
cried.

"What?"

"Gold!" and Hal's voice changed to a
whisper. "That tramp knows there's gold
on this island, and he's trying to dig it up
so you won't know it. He's after gold—
that's what he is!"

"Oh!" gasped Jan, her eyes shining
brightly.

"Oh!" exclaimed Ted. "Can't we stop
him? This is grandpa's island. He mustn't
take grandpa's gold."

"There's only one way to stop him," said Hal quickly.

"How?" demanded Ted and Janet in the same breath.

"We'll have to dig for the gold ourselves! Come on, let's get some shovels and we'll start right away. It must be up near the cave. Come on! We'll dig for the gold ourselves!"

CHAPTER XV

THE BIG HOLE

HAL CHESTER was very much in earnest. His eyes shone and he could not keep still. He fairly danced around Janet and Ted.

"Do you really think that tramp-man was looking for gold?" asked Ted.

" 'Deed I do," declared Hal. "What else was he after?"

Neither Ted nor Janet could answer that.

"But how will we know where it is?" asked Janet. "We don't know where there's any gold, and mother won't want us to go near that tramp-man."

"And I don't want to, either," answered Hal. "But we can dig down till we find the gold, can't we?"

"If we knowed—I mean if we knew where to dig," agreed Ted, after thinking about it. "But digging for gold isn't like digging for angle-worms to go fishing. You can dig them anywhere. But you've got to have a gold mine to dig for gold."

"Well, we'll start a mine," decided Hal. "That's what the miners do out West. I read about it in a book at the Home when I was crippled and couldn't walk much. The miners just start to dig, and if they don't find gold in one place they dig in another. That's what we'll do. We'll dig till we find the gold, then we'll have a gold mine."

"Oh, yes, let's do it!" cried Jan. "I'd love to have some gold to make a pair of bracelets for my doll."

"Pooh!" scoffed Ted, "if we get gold we aren't going to waste it on doll's bracelets! Are we, Hal?"

"Well, if Jan helps us dig she can have her share of the gold. That's what miners always do. They divide up the gold and each one takes his share. Of course Jan can do what she likes with hers."

"There, see, Mr. Smarty!" cried Jan to her brother. "I'll make my gold into doll's bracelets."

"Maybe you won't get any," objected Ted.

"Well, I'll help you dig, anyhow. I helped grandpa dig trenches around the

The Big Hole 177

tents so the rain water would run off, and I can help dig a gold mine. I know where the shovels are."

"Good!" cried Hal.

"We don't want any girls in this gold mine!" objected Ted, as his sister hurried off to where Grandpa Martin kept the shovels, hoes and other garden tools he used about the camp.

Usually Ted did not mind what game his sister played with him, but since Hal had spoken of gold the little Curlytop boy had acted differently.

"We don't want girls in the gold mine," repeated Ted.

"Course we do!" laughed Hal. "Jan's a strong digger, and I can't do very much, as my foot that used to be lame isn't all well yet. It used to be almost as strong as the other, but now it isn't. So you and Jan will have to do most of the digging, though I can shovel away the dirt. Anyhow they always have girls or women in gold camps, you know."

"They do?" cried Ted.

"Of course! They do the cooking where there aren't any Chinamen. Mostly Chinamen do the cooking in gold camps, but we haven't any, so we'll have to have a girl. She can be Jan."

"There's a Chinaman who washes shirts and collars in our town," remarked Ted. "Maybe we could get him to cook for us."

"No! What's the use when we've got Jan? Anyhow it'll be only make-believe cooking, and I don't guess that shirt-Chinaman would want to come here just for that. Anyhow we'd have to pay him and we haven't any money."

"We'll get some out of the gold mine," Ted answered.

"Well, maybe we won't find any gold for a week or so."

"Does it take as long as that?"

"Oh, yes. Sometimes longer. And that Chinaman would want to be paid for his cooking every week, or every night maybe. We won't have to pay Jan."

"That's so. Well, then I guess she can come. But we can get my mother or Nora to make us sandwiches and we won't have to cook much of anything."

"That's what I thought, Teddy. But we can let Jan set the table and things like that when she isn't digging. She'll help a lot."

"Yes, she's almost as strong as I am,"

The Big Hole

agreed Ted. "Hurry up, Jan!" he called. "Got those shovels yet?"

"Yes, but I can't carry 'em all. You must help. Come on!"

Jan was walking back toward the boys, dragging two heavy shovels. Seeing this, Hal hurried to help her and Ted followed. They got another shovel and a hoe and with these they started off toward the cave, about which Ted had told Hal.

"That'll be the place where the gold is," decided the visitor. "The tramps must have been looking for it there. We'll start our gold mine right near the cave."

"What about something to eat?" asked Ted, pausing as they started up the path that led to the hole out of which the cave opened.

"That's so. We ought to have something. I'm getting hungry now," remarked Jan, though it was not long since they had had a meal.

"So'm I," announced Ted.

"Better not stop to go back for anything to eat now," decided Hal. "Your mother or grandma might make us stay in camp. Did you tell them we were going to dig for gold, Jan?"

"No. I didn't see any of them when I got the shovels."

"Well then, we'll go on up to the cave. One of us can come back later and get something to eat. They call it 'grub' in the books."

"Call what grub?" Ted asked.

"Stuff the miners eat. We'll send Jan back for the grub after we start the gold mine. You're going to be the cook," Hal informed Ted's sister.

"I am not!" she cried, dropping her shovel. "I'm going to be a gold miner just like you two. If I can't be that I won't play, and I'll take my shovel right back! So there now!"

"Oh, you can be a gold miner too," Hal made haste to say. "But we've got to have a cook—they always do in a gold camp."

"Well, I'll be a cook when I'm not digging gold," agreed Jan. "But I want to get enough for my doll's bracelets."

"That's all right," agreed Hal. It would not do to have Jan leave them right at the start.

If Mrs. Martin or grandpa saw the children starting out with hoe and shovels they probably thought the Curlytops were only going to dig fish worms, as they often did. Grandpa Martin was very fond of fishing, but he did not like to dig the bait. But Trouble was fretful that day, and his mother had to take care of him, so she did not pay much attention to Jan or Ted, feeling sure they would come to no harm.

So on the three children hurried toward the hole into which Ted had fallen just before they found the queer cave.

"This is just the place for a gold mine!" cried Hal when he looked at the ground around the big hole. "I guess some one must have started a mine here once before."

"It does look so," agreed Ted.

"Let's go into the cave," proposed the visitor.

"No, grandpa told us we must never go in without him," objected Jan. "It's all right to stay outside here and dig, but we mustn't go inside. The tramps might be in there."

"That's right," chimed in Ted. "We'll stay outside."

Hal was not very anxious, himself, to go into the dark hole, so they looked at the place where Ted had fallen through the loose leaves and talked about whether it would be better to start to make that hole larger or begin a new one. The children decided the last would be the best thing to do.

"We'll start a new mine of our own," said Hal. "I guess maybe somebody dug there and couldn't find any gold. So we'll start a new mine."

This suited the Curlytops and they soon began making the dirt fly with shovels and hoe, digging a hole that was large enough for all three of them to stand in. Hal said they didn't want to start by making too small a mine.

"If we've got to divide it into three parts we want each one's part big enough to see," he said, and Ted and Jan agreed to this.

The ground was of sand and very easy to dig. There were no big rocks, only a few small stones, and of course this was just what the children liked. So that in about half an hour they had really dug quite a deep hole. It was almost as easy digging as it is in the sand at the seashore, and if any of you have been there you know how soon, even if you use only a big clam shell for a shovel, you can make a hole deep enough for you and your playmates to stand up in.

"Do you see any gold yet?" asked Jan of the two boys, when they had dug down so that only the top parts of their bodies were out of the big hole.

"No, not yet. But we'll come to it pretty soon," Hal said.

"Say, how're we going to get up when the hole gets too deep?" asked Ted. "We ought to have a ladder or something."

"There's a ladder in camp," answered Jan. "Grandpa had it when he put up our real rope swing. Don't you remember, Ted?"

"Yes, that's right. We'd better get it if we're going any deeper, Hal," he added.

"Course we're going deeper. Gold mines are real deep. I guess the ladder would be a good thing."

"Then we'll go for it. Jan, you can come and get us something to eat, too. I'm awful hungry."

"So'm I," said Hal.

While Jan was in the tent-kitchen begging Nora for some cookies and sandwiches, Ted and Hal carried the small ladder, which was not very heavy, up to the big hole they had started. By putting one end of the ladder down inside, allowing it to slant up to the top of the hole, the children could easily get down in and climb up.

After they had eaten the things Jan got from Nora, they began digging again. The hole was soon so deep that the dirt which was shoveled and hoed away from the bottom and sides could no longer be tossed out by Ted and Jan.

"We've got to get a pail and hoist up the dirt," decided Hal. "That's what they do in gold mines. One of us must stay at the bottom and dig the dirt and fill the pail, and the other pull it up by a rope."

"We'll take turns," said Teddy.

"And I want to help, too!" cried Jan, so the boys agreed to let her, especially as they had seen that she could dig and toss dirt almost as well as they could. They found an old pail and part of a clothes-line for the rope, and the work at the "gold mine," as they called it, went on more merrily than before.

By this time the hole was really quite deep —so deep that Hal Chester could not see over the rim when he stood up straight on the bottom, and only by using the ladder could the children get down and up.

"We ought to find gold pretty soon now," said Hal, as he climbed up to let Ted take a turn at going down in the hole and digging.

The Big Hole 185

Just then from the camp they heard the sound of the supper bell.

"Come on!" called Ted, not waiting to go down into the big hole. "We can dig some more after supper and to-morrow. I'm hungry!"

"So'm I," agreed Hal.

Leaving their shovels and the hoe on the pile of dirt, the children hastened down to the tent where Nora had supper waiting for them, and it had a most delicious smell.

"Where have you children been?" asked Mrs. Martin.

"Oh, havin' fun," answered Ted.

"Don't forget your 'g,' Curlytop," warned his mother with a laugh. "Are you hungry, Hal?"

"Indeed I am! This island is a good place for getting hungry."

"And this is a good place to be stopped from getting hungry," laughed Grandpa Martin, as he pulled his chair up to the well-filled table near which Nora stood ready to serve the meal.

The Curlytops and Hal had just a little idea that the grown folks would not like their plan of digging a gold mine, so nothing was said about it. Hal, Ted and Jan looked at one another when their plates were emptied, and then all three of them started once more back toward the big hole.

"Where are you going?" asked Mother Martin.

"We——" began Jan, then stopped.

"Oh, we—we're playing a game," answered Ted. It was a sort of game.

"Can't you take Trouble with you? You haven't looked after him to-day," went on Mrs. Martin, "and I want to help Nora. Take Trouble with you."

"All right," agreed Ted, though he thought perhaps Baby William might be in the way at the gold mine.

"Where is he?" asked Jan.

They looked around for the little fellow. He was not in sight.

"He got down from the table and was playing over there on the path a while ago," said Grandpa Martin, and he pointed toward the path that led to the gold mine. But Trouble was not in sight now.

"He must have wandered off into the woods," said his mother. "I've kept him close by me all day, and he didn't like it. Trouble! William!" she called aloud. "Where are you?"

The Big Hole

Ted and Jan looked at one another. Hal seemed startled. The same thought came to all three of them:

"Suppose Trouble had fallen down the big hole at the gold mine?"

CHAPTER XVI

A GLAD SURPRISE

Janet, Ted and Hal started to run.

"Where are you going?" called Mrs. Martin after them. "Wait for Trouble!"

"We're going to find him," answered Janet.

"Maybe he fell down the big hole we dug for a gold mine," added Ted.

"What do you mean?" gasped Mrs. Martin.

"What have you Curlytops been up to now?" asked Grandpa Martin.

"We dug a big hole to find the gold the tramps are looking for on this island," explained Hal, who walked on slowly, following Mrs. Martin, who had run after Ted and Janet. "Maybe the little boy fell into it."

"Where did you dig the big hole?" asked grandpa, and he, too, began to be afraid that something had happened.

A Glad Surprise

"Up near what Ted calls the cave. It's got a ladder in it, our gold mine hole has, and maybe Trouble could climb out on that."

"If it's a hole deep enough for a ladder, I'm afraid he couldn't," said Grandpa Martin. "You children must have dug a pretty big hole."

"We wanted to find the gold," explained Hal.

"What gold?"

"The gold the tramps are looking for here on Star Island. Ted told me about them, and I suppose they were after gold. We want to find it first."

"There isn't any gold here, and you mustn't dig holes so deep that Trouble —or anyone else—would wander off and fall into them," said Mr. Martin. "However, I presume it will be all right. But we must hurry there and find out what has happened."

He and Hal hastened on, following Mrs. Martin and the Curlytops, who were now out of sight around a turn in the path that led to the big hole. Hal was rather frightened, for he knew it was his idea, more than the plans of Jan and Ted, that had caused the "gold mine" to be dug.

On and on, along the path and up the hill hurried grandpa and Mrs. Martin and the children. They called aloud for Trouble, but he did not answer. At least they could not hear him if he did. He must have gone quietly away from the table when no one noticed him. He had had his supper before the Curlytops and Hal came from their digging.

"There's the pile of dirt," called back Ted, who was running on ahead. He pointed to the mound of yellow sand that he, Hal and Jan had dug out of the hole.

"And some one is there, digging!" cried Jan. "Oh, maybe it's Trouble!"

"I only hope he hasn't fallen in and hurt himself!" murmured Mrs. Martin.

By this time Grandpa Martin and Hal had caught up to the others. They could all see some one making the dirt fly on top of the yellow mound of sand at one side of the big hole.

As Ted came nearer he saw a man on top of the dirt, using a shovel. The man was digging quickly, and at first Teddy thought it was one of the tramps. But a second look showed him he was wrong. And then came a glad surprise, for the man called:

A Glad Surprise

"I'll have him out in a minute. He isn't under very deep!"

"Why it's the lollypop man!" cried Jan.

And so it was, Mr. Sander, the jolly, fat man who sold waffles and lollypops.

"Is Trouble in the hole? Are you digging him out?" gasped Mrs. Martin, and she felt as though she were going to faint, she said afterward.

"No! Trouble isn't here—I mean he isn't in the hole!" cried Mr. Sander. "It's your goat, Nicknack, who's buried under the sand. But his nose is sticking out so he won't smother, and I'll soon have him all the way out."

"But where is Trouble?" cried Baby William's mother.

"There he is, safe and sound, tied to a tree so he can't get in the way of the dirt I'm shoveling out. I didn't want to throw sand in his eyes!" cried the lollypop man. "Trouble is all right!"

And so the little fellow was, though he had been crying, perhaps from fright, and his face was tear-streaked and dirty. But he was safe.

With a glad cry his mother loosed the rope by which Mr. Sander had carefully tied

Trouble to a near-by tree and gathered him up in her arms.

Meanwhile Grandpa Martin caught up one of the shovels and began to help the lollypop man dig in the sand. The Curlytops and Hal saw what had happened. A lot of the dirt they had shoveled out had slid back into the big hole, almost filling it. And caught under this dirt was Nicknack, their goat. Only the black tip of his nose stuck out, and it is a good thing this much of him was uncovered, or he might have smothered under the sand.

"How did it happen?" asked Ted.

"There must have been a cave-in at our gold mine," said Hal.

"But how did Nicknack get here?" Ted went on.

"I guess Trouble must have untied him and brought him here." suggested Janet.

Then they all watched while Grandpa Martin and the lollypop man dug out the goat.

"Baa-a-a-a-a!" bleated Nicknack as he scrambled out after most of the sand had been shoveled off his back. "Baa-a-a-a!"

"My! I guess he's glad to get out!" cried Ted.

A Glad Surprise

"I guess so!" agreed the lollypop man. "I got here just as the dirt caved in on him, and I began to dig as soon as I tied Trouble out of the way so he'd be safe."

"But how did you come to be here?" asked Grandpa Martin.

"And how did our goat get here?" asked Janet.

"I saw Trouble leading him along by the strap on his horns," explained Mr. Sander. "I guess he must have taken him out of his stable when you folks weren't looking. Trouble led the goat up on top of the pile of sand near the hole. I called to him to be careful.

"Just as I did so the sand slid down and I saw the goat go down into the hole. Baby William fell down, but he didn't slide in with the dirt. Then I ran and picked him up, and I tied him to the tree with a piece of rope I found fast to a pail. I thought that was the best way to keep him out of danger while I dug out the goat."

"I guess it was," said Grandpa Martin.

"Poor Trouble cried when I tied him fast, but I knew crying wouldn't hurt him, and falling under a lot of sand might. I dug as fast as I could, for I knew how you Curlytops loved your goat. He's all right, I guess."

And Nicknack was none the worse for having been buried under the sliding sand. As they learned afterward Trouble had slipped off to have some fun by himself with the pet animal. Baby William had, somehow, found his way to the "gold mine," and pretending the pile of sand was a mountain had led Nicknack up it. Then had come the slide down into the big hole which Hal and the Curlytops had dug. If it had not been for Mr. Sander appearing when he did, poor Nicknack might have died.

"But, Trouble. You must never, never, never go away again alone with Nicknack!" warned Mother Martin. "Never! Do you hear?"

"Me won't!" promised the little fellow.

"And you children mustn't dig any more deep holes," said Grandpa Martin. "There isn't any gold on this island, so don't look for it."

"But what are the tramps looking for?" Ted asked.

"I can't tell you. But, no matter about that, don't dig any more deep holes. They're dangerous!"

"We won't!" promised the Curlytops and Hal.

"How did you come to pay a visit to Star Island, Mr. Sander?" asked the children's mother.

"Well, I'm stopping for the night on the main shore just across from here," was the answer, "so, having had my supper and having made my bed in my red wagon, I thought I'd come over and pay you a visit. I heard you were camping here, so I borrowed a boat and rowed over. I walked along this path, and I happened to see Trouble and the goat. Then I knew I had found the right place, but I did not imagine I'd have to come to the rescue of my friend Nicknack," and with a laugh he patted the shaggy coat of the animal, that rubbed up against the kind lollypop man.

"Well, come back to the tent and visit a while," was Grandpa Martin's invitation. "We're ever so much obliged to you."

"What does all this mean about tramps and a gold mine?" asked Mr. Sander. "If there's gold to be had in an easier way than by selling hot waffles from a red wagon with a white horse to pull it, I'd like to know about it," he added with a jolly laugh.

"Oh, ho! Oh, ho!" he cried. "Hot waffles do I sell. Hot waffles I love well!"

"Did you bring any with you?" asked Ted eagerly.

"Indeed I did, my little Curlytop. They may not be hot now, but maybe your mother can warm them on the stove," and picking up a package he had laid down near the tree to which he had tied Trouble, the lollypop man gave it to Mrs. Martin with a low bow.

"Waffles for the Curlytops," he said laughing.

CHAPTER XVII

TROUBLE'S PLAYHOUSE

SAFE once more in their camp, the children ate the waffles which Nora made nice and crisp again over the fire. Trouble was comforted and made happy by two of the sugar-covered cakes, and then everyone told told his or her share in what had just happened.

"So you think there are gold-hunting tramps here?" asked the lollypop man, just before he got ready to go back to the mainland where he had left his red wagon and white horse.

"Well, there are ragged men here—tramps I suppose you could call them," answered Grandpa Martin. "But I don't know anything about gold. That's one of Hal's ideas."

"I couldn't think of anything else they'd be looking for," explained Ted's friend.

"Don't you think it might be gold, Mr. Martin?"

"Hardly—on this island. Anyhow we haven't seen the ragged men lately, so they may have gone. Perhaps they were only stray fishermen. We would like to thank one for having pulled Trouble out of the spring, only we haven't had the chance."

"No. He ran away without stopping for thanks," said Baby William's mother. "He must be a kind man, even if he is a tramp."

After a little more talk while they were seated about the campfire Grandpa Martin built in front of the tents, during which time the lollypop man told of his travels since he had helped sell the cherries for the chewing candy, Mr. Sander rowed back to the main shore to sleep in his red wagon, which was like a little house on wheels.

"Come again!" invited Mrs. Martin.

"I will when any more goats fall into gold mines," he promised with a laugh.

The next day Grandpa Martin filled up the hole Ted, Jan and Hal had dug, thus making sure that neither Trouble nor anyone else, not even Nicknack the goat, would again fall down into it. For when the sand slid into the "gold mine," carrying the goat

Trouble's Playhouse 199

with it, the hole was not altogether filled. Then Grandpa Martin brought away the hoe and shovels, and told the children they must play at some other game.

"Where are you going now?" called Mrs. Martin to the two Curlytops, as they started away from camp one morning. Hal stayed in the tent, as he was tired.

"Oh, we're just going for a walk," answered Teddy.

"We want to have some fun," added his sister.

"Well, don't go digging any more gold mines," warned Grandpa Martin, with a laugh. "All the fun of camping will be spoiled if you get into that sort of trouble again."

"We won't," promised Janet, and Teddy nodded his head to show that he, too, would at least try to be good.

It was not that the Curlytops were bad— that is, any worse than perhaps you children are sometimes, or, perhaps, some boys or girls you know of. They were just playful and full of life, and wanted to be doing something all the while.

"Do you want to take Trouble with you?" asked Mrs. Martin, as Ted and Janet started away from camp, and down a woodland path.

"Yes, we'll take him," said Janet. "Come on, little brother," she went on. "Come with sister and have some fun."

"Only I can't play in de dirt 'cause I got on a clean apron," said Baby William.

"No, we won't let you play in the dirt," Teddy remarked. "But don't fall down, either. That's where he gets so dirty," Teddy told his mother. "He's always falling down, Trouble is."

"It—it's so—s'ippery in de woods!" said the little fellow.

"So it is—on the pine needles," laughed Grandpa Martin, who was going to the mainland in the boat. But this time he did not want to take the children with him. "It is slippery in the woods, Trouble, my boy. But keep tight hold of Jan's hand, and maybe you won't fall down."

"Me will," said Trouble, but he did not mean that he would fall down. He meant he would keep tight hold of Jan's hand. Then he started off by her side, with Ted walking on ahead, ready for anything he might see that would make fun for him and his sister.

Trouble calling, and his voice sounded very strange.

"Oh, what has happened to him now?" cried Janet.

"We'd better go to see!" exclaimed Teddy.

They ran back to where they had left their little brother. All they could see of him was his back and legs. He did not seem to have any head.

"Oh! Oh!" gasped Janet. "Where is Trouble's head?"

Ted did not know, and said so, and then the little fellow cried:

"Tum an' det me out! Tum an' det me out!"

Then Janet saw what had happened. Trouble had thrust his head between the crotch, or the Y-shaped part, of a tree, and had become so tightly wedged that he could not get out.

"Oh, what shall we do?" cried Janet.

"I'll show you," answered Teddy. "You can help me." Then he pushed on the little boy's head, and Janet pulled, and he was soon free again, a little scratched about the neck, and frightened, but not hurt.

"You must never do such a thing again,"

said Mrs. Martin, when the children reached camp and told her what had happened.

"No, we won't do it any more," promised Trouble, feeling of his neck, where he had thrust it between the parts of the tree.

"And you mustn't go off again, and leave him by himself," said their mother to the Curlytops. "There is no telling what he'll do."

"That's right," said Grandpa Martin with a laugh. "You may go away, leaving Trouble standing on his feet, but when you come back he's standing on his head. Oh, you're a great bunch of trouble!" and he caught the little fellow up in his arms and kissed him.

For several days Teddy and Janet and Hal had many good times on Star Island. Then they wanted something new for amusement.

"Let's make a trap and catch something," said Ted, after he and Jan had spoken of several ways of having fun.

"How can you make a trap?" Hal asked.

"I'll show you," offered Ted. "You just take a box, turn it upside down, and raise one end by putting a stick under it. Then you tie a string to the stick, and when you pull the string the stick is yanked out and the box falls down and you catch something."

"What do you catch?" Hal asked.

"Oh, birds, or an animal—maybe a fox or a muskrat—whatever goes under the box when it's raised up."

"But what makes them go under?" Hal inquired.

"To get something to eat. You see you put some bait under the box—some crumbs for birds or pieces of meat for a fox or a muskrat. Then you hide in the bushes, with the end of the string in your hand and when you see anything right under the box you pull it and catch 'em!"

"Oh, but doesn't it hurt them?" asked Hal, who had a very kind heart.

"Maybe it might, Ted," put in Jan.

"No. It doesn't hurt 'em a bit," declared Ted. "They just stay under the box, you know, like in a cage."

"I wouldn't like to catch a bird," said Hal softly. "You see the birds are friends of Princess Blue Eyes. She wouldn't like to have them caught."

"Oh, well, we could let them go again," Ted decided, after a little thought.

"Does Princess Blue Eyes like foxes and muskrats too?" Jan asked softly.

"I guess she likes everything—birds, animals and flowers. Anyway I make-believe she does," and Hal smiled. "Of course she's only a pretend-person, but I like to think she's real. I like to dream of her."

"I would, too," said Janet softly. "We mustn't catch any birds, Ted, nor animals, either."

"Not if we let them go right off quick?" Ted asked.

"No," and Janet shook her head. "It might scare 'em you know. And the box might fall on their legs, or their wings, if it's a bird, and hurt them."

"Well, then, we won't do it!" decided Ted. "I wouldn't want to hurt anything, and I wouldn't want to make your friend, Princess Blue Eyes, feel bad," he added to Hal. He remembered the story Hal had told about the make-believe Princess, when they sat in the green meadow studded with yellow buttercups and white daisies.

"Let's play store!" suggested Jan. "There's lots of pretty stones and shells on the shore, and we can use them for money."

"What'll we sell?" asked Hal.

"Oh, we can sell other stones—big ones—for bread, and sand for sugar and leaves for cookies and things like that," Janet proposed.

"I wish we had something real to eat, and then we could sell that and it would be some good," remarked Ted. "I'm going to ask Nora."

"Oh, that'll be fun!" cried Jan. "Come on, Hal. We'll get the store ready and Ted can go in and ask Nora for some real cookies and maybe a piece of cake."

Nora, good-natured as she always was, gave Ted a nice lot of broken cookies, some crackers and some lumps of sugar so the children could play store and really eat the things they sold. Hal gathered some mussel shells and colored stones on the shore of the lake, and these were money.

The store counter was made by putting a board across two boxes and they took turns being the storekeeper. Trouble wanted to play, too. But he only wanted to buy bits of molasses cookies, and he ate the pieces as fast as he got them, without pretending to go out of the store to take them home.

"Me buy more tookie!" he would say, swallowing the last crumb and hurrying up to the board counter with another "penny," which was a shell or a stone.

"You mustn't eat them up so fast, Trouble," said Janet. "Else we won't have any left to play store with."

"Oh, well, we can get more from Nora," said Ted. "And the cookies taste awful good."

They played store until there were no more good things left to eat and Nora would not hand out any others from her boxes and pans in the kitchen tent. Then the Curlytops and Hal got in the rowboat and paddled about in the shallow cove.

Trouble did not go with them, his mother saying he must have a little sleep so he would not be so cross in the afternoon. And when Jan, her brother and Hal came up from the lake they found the little fellow making what he called a "playhouse."

"Oh, what funny stones Trouble has!" cried Ted as he saw them. "They're blue."

"They're pretty," decided Janet. "Where'd you get them, Trouble?"

"Over dere," and he pointed to a spot some distance from the camp.

"He found them himself and brought them here in his apron," said Mrs. Martin.

"He's been piling them up into what I called a castle, but he says it's a playhouse. He's been very good playing with the blue stones."

"Let's get some too, and see who can build the biggest castle!" cried Janet. "Show us where you got them, Trouble."

But when Baby William toddled to the place where he had picked up the blue stones there were no more. He had gathered them all, it seemed, and now would not let his brother or sister take any from his pile.

However they found other stones which did as well, though they were not blue in color, and soon the Curlytops and Hal, as well as Trouble, were making a little house of stones.

"This is more fun than playing store!" cried Janet, as she made a little round tower as part of her castle.

"Are you making a palace for Princess Blue Eyes, Hal?" asked Ted.

"Yes," he answered, for his stone castle was rather a large one. "But I can't be sure she'll like it. She doesn't want to stay in one place very long. She's like a firefly—always dancing about."

And so they pretended and played, having

a very good time, while Mother Martin watched them and smiled. The children were having great fun camping with grandpa.

The castles finished—Trouble's being the prettiest because of the blue stones, though not as large or fancy as the others—the Curlytops, Hal and Baby William went on a little picnic in the woods that afternoon, taking Nicknack with them. Or rather, the goat took them, for he pulled them in the cart along the forest path.

When Jan, Hal and Ted were eating breakfast the next morning they heard a cry from Trouble, who had toddled out of the tent as soon as he had finished his meal.

"Oh, what has happened to him now?" exclaimed Mother Martin. "Run and see, Jan, dear, that's a good girl!"

Janet found her little brother at the place where they had made the castles the night before. Trouble's eyes were filled with tears.

"My p'ayhouse all gone!" he cried. "Trouble's house all goned away!"

It was true. Not a trace of his playhouse was left! In the night someone or something had taken the blue stones away.

CHAPTER XVIII

IN THE CAVE

Trouble felt very bad about his playhouse of blue stones which had been taken away. He was only a little fellow, and when he had gone to so much work, building up what looked like a fairy castle, he surely thought he would find it where he left it at night to have it to play with the next morning. But it was gone.

"All goned," sobbed Trouble.

"Isn't it funny, though?" said Teddy. "Mine is all right, and so is yours, Jan, and Hal's, too. They just spoiled Trouble's."

"Maybe it was Nicknack," suggested Jan. "He might have got loose in the night and knocked it down. But he didn't mean to I guess, for he's a good goat."

"It couldn't have been Nicknack," declared Hal.

"Why not?" asked Ted. "Didn't he fall

down into the big hole when Trouble led him to it?"

"Yes, but Nicknack is there in his stable. He isn't loose at all, and he'd have to be loose to come here and knock over Trouble's playhouse. The goat is tied fast just where he was last night."

So Nicknack was; and Grandpa Martin, who was the first one up in the camp that morning, said the goat was lying quietly down in his stable when he went to give him a drink of water. So it couldn't have been Nicknack.

"Anyhow, Trouble's blue-stone castle wasn't just knocked down," went on Hal, "it's gone—every stone is gone. Somebody took 'em!"

Jan and Ted noticed this for the first time. When Trouble had called out that his playhouse was gone they had thought he meant it was just knocked over. But, instead, it was gone completely. Not a blue stone was left.

And, strangely enough, none of the other three castles was touched. Hal had built quite a large one, but not a stone had been taken from it.

"Where my p'ayhouse?" asked Trouble,

In the Cave 213

looking all about. "I want my p'ayhouse."

"We'll find it for you," promised Jan, though she did not know how she was going to do it. Perhaps Hal could think of a way. Hal was older than Jan and Ted.

"What's the matter, Curlytops?" asked Mother Martin as she came out of the tent. "Has anything happened? Why is Trouble crying? Did he get hurt?"

"No, but someone took away his nice blue stone castle," explained Jan, and she and the others took turns telling what had happened.

"It is queer," said Grandpa Martin, when he came up and heard what had taken place. "I wonder if any of those——"

Then he stopped talking and looked at the children's mother in a queer way. She nodded her head, glanced down at the Curlytops and Hal, and put her finger across her lips as your teacher does in school when she wants someone to stop whispering.

Hal saw what Mrs. Martin did, but neither Jan nor Ted noticed, for they were running around looking for any of the blue stones that might have been scattered from Trouble's playhouse.

"Never mind," said Mother Martin. "I'll

find you something else to play with, Trouble. You shall have a nice ride with Nicknack. You'll take him, won't you, Jan and Ted?"

"Yes," they answered.

"I want my p'ayhouse!" sobbed Baby William, and for a time he made a fuss about his missing blue stones.

"I guess I know what happened to them," said Hal in a whisper to Jan and Ted when their mother had taken Trouble into the tent to find something with which to amuse him.

"What?" asked Ted in a whisper.

"The tramps!" exclaimed Hal, looking over his shoulder to make sure no one but his two little friends heard him. "That's what your grandfather was going to say the time he stopped so quick. Your mother didn't want him to speak of them. But I'm sure the tramps took the blue stones from Trouble's castle."

"What would they do with 'em?" Ted demanded.

"There's gold in 'em!" whispered Hal, more excited than ever now. "There's gold in those blue stones, and the tramps know it. That's what they've been looking for, and when Trouble had 'em all in a nice pile

In the Cave 215

made into a playhouse, the tramps came along in the night and took 'em away."

"Oh, do you s'pose it could happen that way, really?" asked Jan, her eyes big with wonder.

"Course it could!" said Hal, growing more excited all the while. "I remember now, gold doesn't always look yellow when you find it, the way it does in a watch or a ring. Sometimes gold is inside stones and they have to melt 'em in the fire to get the gold out. My nurse at the Crippled Home read me about it. And there was gold in the blue stones. That's why the tramps came and got 'em—I mean *them*," and he corrected himself. "They told me not to say 'em,' " he added with a smile.

"Do you really think the blue stones had gold in 'em—them?" asked Ted.

"Yes, I do! Else why would the tramps want them? They came last night and took Trouble's castle—every stone, and now they've hid the gold away."

"Where?" asked Jan, as excited as the boys.

"I think it must be up in the cave," went on Hal. "If we could only go there and look we could find it too. Let's go."

"Maybe mother wouldn't let us." suggested Ted.

"We don't have to tell her," said Jan.

"I don't mean to do anything bad, nor have you," went on Hal. "But wouldn't it be great if we could go up to the cave, without anybody knowing it, and get the gold? Then your mother would be glad, and your grandpa, too."

"Maybe they would—if there was gold in the blue stones," agreed Ted.

"We could pretend there was," said Janet. "Wouldn't that be fun? But I don't want to go into that dark cave 'cept maybe grandpa goes, too, with a light."

"You wouldn't be afraid with us, would you?" asked Hal.

"Hal and I would be with you," added Ted.

"Well, maybe I wouldn't be afraid if you took hold of my hands. But it's dark there —awful dark."

"I've got one of those little electric lights," Hal said. "My father sent it to me for my birthday when I was in the Home, and I didn't use it hardly at all, 'cause I wasn't up nights. It flashes bright. I brought it with me when I came to visit you,

In the Cave

and I can get it and take it to the cave with us."

"That'll be fun!" cried Ted. "Let's go, Jan!" he pleaded.

"Well, maybe I will. But hadn't we better ask mother?"

"Maybe she'd say we couldn't," suggested her brother, speaking very slowly. "We'll tell her when we come back."

Of course this was not just the right thing to do, especially after Ted and his sister had been told not to go to the cave alone. But they forgot all about that when Hal spoke about gold being in the blue stones. Ted and Jan thought it would be wonderful if they could get some gold for their mother and grandfather, who was not as rich as he had been, even if he did sell a lot of cherries.

"We can't take Trouble along," said Jan, as she saw her little brother coming out of the tent. "We've got to leave him here."

"Yes," agreed Hal. "But we don't need to go right away. We can play with him awhile. You and Ted take care of Trouble and I'll go to get my flashlight. I put it under my pillow last night."

"And I'll get something to eat from Nora," added Ted. "We'll make-believe we're going on a little picnic in the woods."

"Oh, that'll be fun!" cried Jan. She was not afraid to think of the dark cave now.

"Trouble want p'ayhouse!" cried Baby William, as he toddled up to his sister. "Want b'ue stones."

"I can't get you the blue stones—not now," said Janet. "But I guess Teddy will let you knock down his playhouse and build up another one. And you can knock down my playhouse, too. Come on, Trouble!"

Knocking over the playhouses of stone which his brother and sister had built the night before seemed such great fun to the little boy, and he had such a good time doing this and, with Jan's help, making another and larger house of his own, that he forgot all about his blue stones.

Ted and Hal did not forget them, though, and the more they thought of the queer way they had been taken away in the night, the more they felt sure that the stones must have gold in them, or, at least, something that the tramps wanted badly enough to come and take it.

And that it was the tramps, or some man, or men, who had taken the blue stones, Hal and Ted felt certain.

"For no dog or other animal could carry away every stone," said Hal. "Anyhow a dog wouldn't want them, nor a fox either. It was the tramps all right."

"Maybe they wouldn't like us to go to the cave and get the stones back," suggested Ted.

"Well, the tramps can't have the blue stones," said Hal, shaking his head. "We found 'em, and they're Trouble's. But he's so little he don't want any gold, so we'll give it to your grandfather and grandmother."

"Don't you want any?" asked Ted.

"No. My father's got lots of money. I just want to find some gold for you. I got my light from under my pillow," and Hal showed it to Ted. They were out behind the sleeping tent talking, and Ted had his pockets full of cookies and little cakes he had begged from Nora.

"Though what in the world the child is going to do with them all, is more than I can guess," laughed the maid. "But I s'pose the children are always hungry."

Ted and Hal were now ready to go to the cave. They looked around the corner of the tent and saw Janet still playing with Trouble. He had gotten over crying for his blue stones, and was now busy making a playhouse of the rocks and pebbles his brother and sister had used.

"Come on, Janet! We're going!" called Ted in a loud whisper, as his sister looked at him. He also made motions with his hands to show that he and Hal were ready to start for the cave.

Janet saw that her little brother was too busy playing to need her to stay with him—at least for a time. Still she could not leave him alone without calling her mother or Nora to watch what he did.

Very quietly, while Baby William was trying to make one stone stay on top of another in one side of the castle he was making, Janet stepped up to the flap of the tent, inside which her mother was sitting sewing.

"I'm going with Ted and Hal into the woods," said the little girl. "Will you watch Trouble, Mother?"

"Yes, Janet. But be careful, and don't go too far."

Janet did not answer but hurried away. Of course she did not do just right, for she knew her mother would not want her to go to the cave, nor would Mrs. Martin have let Ted and Hal go had she known it. But the

HAL WALKED BOLDLY INTO THE DARK CAVE.

The Curlytops on Star Island   Page 224

In the Cave

Curlytops and Hal were very desirous of finding the blue stones and of seeing if there was any gold in them, and they did not stop to think of what was right and what was wrong.

"Hurry up now!" exclaimed Hal as he went on ahead up the path that led from behind the tents to the queer cave. "We want to get there before anybody knows it."

"What'll we do if the tramps are there?" asked Ted.

"They won't be there," said Hal, though how he could tell that he did not say.

"I've got a little hatchet and we can cut down some clubs," said Ted. He had brought with him a little Boy Scout hatchet, with a covering over the sharp blade. His grandfather had given it to Ted, but had told him never to take it out alone. But Ted did, and this was another wrong thing.

I'm afraid if I speak of all the wrong things the Curlytops did that day I'd never finish with this story. But it wasn't often they did so many acts they ought not to have done.

On they hurried through the woods, the boys hurrying ahead of Janet. She did her best to keep up with them, but her legs were shorter than Ted's or Hal's and it was hard work for the little girl.

"Oh, wait for me!" she called at last. "I'm awful tired."

"Hurry up!" begged Ted. "We want to get the blue stones before the tramps take 'em away!"

"Are they going to?" asked Janet, sitting down on a stone to rest, after she had caught up to the boys.

"Well, they might," answered Hal. "We've got to hurry."

They went on again, walking a little more slowly this time, and when they came to a muddy puddle in the middle of the woodland path, Ted tried to jump over it. But he slipped on the edge and one leg, from his foot to above his knee, got very wet and muddy.

"Oh, wow!" he cried. "Now I've got to stop and clean this off."

He began to wipe off the worst of the mud on bunches of grass, while Janet sat down on a log near by.

"I'm sorry you fell in the mud, Teddy," she said, "but I'm glad I can rest, for I'm awful tired. You go so fast!"

"Come on, hurry up!" called Hal, as Ted

In the Cave

still brushed away with the bunch of grass. "Let it dry and it will come off easier."

"I guess it will," agreed Ted, looking at his muddy stocking. "It won't come off this way."

However, the accident had given his sister a little chance to rest, and now Janet was able to keep up with the boys. Pretty soon they were near the hole into which Ted had fallen, and out of which the cave opened.

"Now be careful!" whispered Hal, as he got out his flashlight. "Maybe the tramps are there!"

"I've got my hatchet!" exclaimed Ted.

"I'm not going in if the tramps are there," declared Janet.

"We'll look first, and see," offered Hal.

"But I don't want to stay here alone!" objected Janet, as her brother and Hal slid down into the hole and looked into the black opening of the cave.

"We won't go very far," promised Ted. "We'll be back in a minute. Don't be afraid."

Then he and Hal went into the cave, while Jan, half wanting to cry, waited outside.

CHAPTER XIX

THE BLUE LIGHT AGAIN

FLASHING his light about, Hal walked boldly into the dark cave. Ted followed, just a little bit afraid, though he did not want to say so.

"Don't go too far," begged Janet's brother. "Jan'll be afraid if we leave her alone."

"I won't go far," promised Hal. "I just want to see if there're any tramps in here."

"Listen an' maybe you can hear them talking," suggested Ted.

Hal, though larger and older than Ted, was not quite brave enough to go very far into the dark cave, even if he did have his light with him. So, after taking a few steps, he stopped and listened. So did Ted.

They could hear nothing but the voice of Janet calling to them from outside.

"Ted! Hal!" cried the little girl.

The Blue Light Again

"Where are you? I'm going back to camp!"

"We're coming!" answered Ted. "Come on back and get her," he added to his chum. "Then we'll look for the blue rocks."

"I guess we can't find them unless they're right around here," returned Hal, as he moved his light about in a circle.

"Why not?" asked Ted.

"Because this cave is so dark, and my flashlamp doesn't give much light. We could hardly see the stones if they were here."

"Then how are we going to get 'em?" Ted demanded.

"I guess we'll have to bring a big lantern. Maybe we ought to bring your grandfather along."

"I guess we had better," agreed Ted. "But we can look a little bit when we're here. Let's go for Janet. She's crying."

Janet was crying by this time, not liking to be left alone outside while the boys were in the cave. They ran back to her and her tears were soon dried.

"Will you come in a little way with us?" asked her brother. "There isn't anything to be afraid of. Is there, Hal?"

"No, not a thing. We won't go in very

far, Jan. And maybe you can see the blue stones. We couldn't, but sometimes girls' eyes are better than boys. Come on!"

So with Hal holding a hand on one side, and Ted on the other, Janet went slowly into the cave with her brother and his chum. Hal flashed his light, and by its gleam the Curlytops could see that the cave was large, larger even than it had seemed when they were in it with their grandfather.

"Look on the floor for the rocks," suggested Hal. "That's where the tramp-man would put 'em if he brought 'em here."

But they did not see the blue rocks, nor any others. The floor of the cave seemed to be of stone or hard clay, and there was nothing on it. They did not go in far enough to see the sacks which Grandpa Martin said someone had used for a bed, nor did the children see the bread and other bits of food which might have meant that someone had had a picnic in the cave.

"I guess the rocks aren't here," said Hal, in disappointed tones as Janet said she wanted to turn back, for she did not like it in the cave. "Or else maybe they're away at the far end."

"I'm not going there!" exclaimed Ted.

"No, I guess we won't go," agreed Hal. "We'll go and tell your grandfather and have him come with a big lantern."

"Hark! What's that?" suddenly called Jan, taking a tighter hold of her brother's hand.

From the back part of the cave came a noise. It was as though a rock had fallen —probably it had—from the roof of the cavern.

"Someone's throwing stones at us!" cried Ted.

"Who? Who? Who?" a voice seemed to ask.

"Oh, dear! We don't know who it was!" cried Janet. "Come on out of here! I'm afraid!"

"That was only an owl," said Hal with a laugh. "Owls live in dark caves in the daytime and when it's dark they hoot and call 'who!' I've heard 'em lots of times around the Home."

"There isn't any cave at the Home," objected Ted, who was as frightened as Janet was.

"No, but there were owls in the trees. I heard 'em lots of times. But we'll go out. I guess maybe that was a loose stone that fell down and made the first noise. But we don't want any to fall on our heads. Come on!" called Hal.

Together he and Ted led Janet back to the mouth of the cave, where they could see the sunshine. And even Hal, who was not so frightened as the Curlytops had been, was glad to get out.

"It's too bad we couldn't find the blue gold-stones," he said. "But maybe the tramps didn't hide them there, anyhow. We'll look around some more."

"Let's eat," suggested Ted. "I'm hungry, and I've got a lot of cookies in my pockets."

So they sat down on a stone in a shady place not far from the cave and ate the things Nora had given Ted. They then got a drink from a bubbling spring not far away, and pretended they were on a picnic.

Ted's muddy stocking had dried by this time, and he and Jan, using sticks, scraped most of the dirt off.

"Now we'd better be going home," Jan suggested after a bit. "There isn't any fun here."

"Yes, we might as well go," agreed Hal. "And I'll tell you what let's do!"

The Blue Light Again

"What?" demanded Ted.

"Let's look in the place where Trouble found those blue stones and see if we can find any more."

"Oh, yes, let's!" cried Janet. She was happy again, now that she was out in the bright sunshine.

The children remembered where Baby William had found the pretty rocks from which he had made his castle, but when they reached the place not a one was to be had, though they searched all about.

"I guess Trouble took them all," said Janet. "I remember now, I helped him look for more and we couldn't find any."

"Well, maybe there'll be some more somewhere else," suggested Hal hopefully. "Let's look."

So they looked, wandering about in the woods not far from camp, until they heard Nora ringing the bell for dinner.

"Well, where have you children been?" asked Mrs. Martin as they came trooping up to the tent, tired, hungry and dirty.

"Oh, we've been looking for gold," explained Ted, but he did not say they had visited the cave, where they had been told not to go.

"You didn't dig any more deep holes, did you?" asked his grandfather.

"No, sir," answered Ted.

After dinner Ted asked Hal why he didn't speak of having Grandpa Martin go to the cave with the big lantern.

"I thought you were going to do that," he said to Hal.

"Well, I was. But maybe we can find some more of the blue stones for ourselves. We'll look around before we ask your grandpa to help."

Janet wanted to stay around camp and play with her dolls that afternoon, and she took care of Trouble.

"Then we'll go for a goat ride," said Ted. "Come on, Hal."

The two boys hitched Nicknack to the wagon, and set off down the island.

"We'll look for some more blue rocks," suggested Hal, and Ted was willing.

On and on the two boys rode, now stopping to look at some pretty flower, again waiting to hear the finish of some bird's song. They looked on both sides of the woodland path for some of the blue rocks, but, though they saw some of other colors, there were none like those they wanted.

The Blue Light Again

"Whoa there, where are you going now?" Ted suddenly called to Nicknack, and the little boy pulled on the reins by which he guided the goat—or "steered" it, as he sometimes called it.

"What's the matter?" asked Hal.

"Nicknack wants to go over that way and I want him to go straight ahead," answered Ted.

"Maybe he sees some of those blue rocks the way he wants to go," suggested Hal.

"Oh, I don't guess so," replied his chum. "I guess he just wants to get some new kind of grass to eat. Whoa, Nicknack, I tell you!" and Teddy pulled as hard as he could on the reins, without hurting his goat, for he never wanted to do that.

But the goat would not go straight down the island path. He kept pulling off to one side, and at last Ted cried:

"Here, Hal, you take hold of the lines and pull with me. Maybe we can steer him around then."

"Can we pull real hard—I mean will the lines break?" asked Hal.

"Oh, no, they're good and strong," answered Ted.

So he and his chum both pulled on the one

rein—the one to get Nicknack's head pointed straight down the path instead of off to one side, but it did no good. The goat knew what he wanted to do, and he was going to do it.

"Look out!" suddenly cried Teddy. "We're going to tip over!"

The next minute the front wheels of the wagon ran up on a little pile of dirt at one side of the path, and the cart gently tilted to one side and then went over with a rattle and a bang.

"There!" laughed Hal, as he rolled out on some soft grass. "We are over, Ted."

"I knew we were going," said Teddy as he, too, laughed and got up. "Whoa there, Nicknack!" he shouted, for the goat was still going on, dragging the overturned wagon after him.

But Nicknack did not stop until he reached a little bush, on which were some green leaves that he seemed to like very much, for he began to chew them.

"That's what he wanted all the while," said Teddy.

"Well, let him eat all he wants, and then he won't be hungry any more and he'll pull us where we want to go," advised Hal.

They did this, after setting the cart up on

The Blue Light Again

its wheels. When Nicknack turned away from the bush, and looked at the two waiting boys, Ted said:

"Well, I guess we can go on now."

"Yes," added Hal, "and I hope we'll find those blue rocks. But I don't believe we're ever going to."

At last, however, when it was getting rather late in the afternoon and Ted had said it was time to go back, Hal, who was driving the goat through a part of the woods they never before had visited, pointed to a big stone buried in the side of a hill and cried:

"Look! Isn't that rock blue, Ted?"

"It does look kind of blue, yes."

"Then it's just what we're looking for. See, there's lots of little blue rocks, too. Let's take some back to camp. Maybe they're the same kind Trouble had, and there may be gold in 'em! Come on."

They piled the rocks, which were certainly somewhat blue in color, into the wagon, and started back with them.

"We found 'em! We found 'em!" they called as they came within sight of the tents. "We got the blue rocks!"

"Well, they're pretty, certainly," said

Grandpa Martin, as he picked up one from the wagon, "but they're no better than any other rocks around here, as far as I can see."

"They've got gold in 'em, Hal says," Ted stated.

"Gold? Oh, no, Curlytop!" laughed his grandfather. "I've told you there is no gold on this island."

"There's *something* in the blue rocks," declared Hal. "Feel how heavy they are— lots heavier than any other stones around here."

"Yes, they are," agreed Grandpa Martin, as he weighed one of the stones in his hand. "There might be some iron in them, but not gold. Look out!" he suddenly called as the stone slipped from his hand. "Look out for your toes!"

Laughing, the Curlytops and Hal jumped back. The blue stone which Grandpa Martin dropped, struck on the edge of the shovel which was out in front of the tent. As the rock hit the steel tool with a clang, something queer happened.

At once the rock began to burn with a curious blue flame, and a yellowish smoke curled up.

"Oh, the rock's on fire!" cried Janet. "The rock's on fire!"

"Yes, and look!" added Ted. "It's burning blue, just like the light we saw on the island one night."

"And how queer it smells!" exclaimed Hal.

"Sulphur!" ejaculated Grandpa Martin.

He and the children looked at the queer blue fire that seemed to come from inside the rock. What could it mean?

CHAPTER XX

THE HAPPY TRAMP

GRANDPA MARTIN stood looking down at the queer, burning rock. The blue fire was flaming up brighter now, and it made a strange light on the faces of the Curlytops and Hal as they gathered about. The sky was cloudy and it was getting dark.

"Oh, what is it? What is it?" asked Ted and Jan.

"It smells just like old-fashioned sulphur matches that my grandmother used to light," said Nora, who had come out, having seen the queer light from the cook-tent.

"And it *is* sulphur that is burning," said Grandpa Martin. "That rock has sulphur in it, not gold, Hal. And it is the sulphur that is burning with the blue fire."

"But what makes it?" asked the children.

Grandpa Martin did not answer for a few seconds. He stood again looking down at the flaming blue rock. Mrs. Martin, who had started to put Trouble to bed early, came out and looked.

"It's like something I once saw in the theater," said the maid. "I don't like it— that blue light. It reminds me of the time our house was struck by lightning—that sulphur smell."

"It is the same smell," said Mr. Martin. "Curlytops, I think you have found something very queer in this blue rock. I don't know just what it is, but we'll find out. See, the stone is burning like a lump of coal now, but with a blue flame instead of red."

"Just like the night we saw the blue fire on the island before we came camping here," said Ted. "Is it the same thing, Grandpa?"

"I don't know. Perhaps it is. Where did you get the blue rocks?"

"Over in the woods," answered Hal. "There's a great big one there. As big as this tent."

"Is there?" some one suddenly asked. "Then please show me where it is! Oh, can it be that at last I have found what I have been looking for so long?"

The Curlytops and the others turned at the sound of this new and strange voice. A man seemed to spring out of the bushes back of the tent. By the light of the blue fire Ted and Jan saw that his clothes were ragged and torn in many places.

"Oh! Oh!" gasped Jan. "That's the tramp!"

"Well, I guess maybe I do look like a tramp, all ragged and dirty as I am," laughed the man, and his voice sounded pleasant. "But I am not a regular tramp. I am Mr. Weston—Alfred Weston," he went on, speaking to Grandpa Martin. "I haven't a card with me, but when I get washed and dressed and shaved I'll look more like what I am. Excuse me for intruding this way, but I could not keep from speaking when I heard what you were talking about."

"Then aren't you a tramp?" asked Ted.

"No, though I have been *tramping* all over this island looking for the very blue rock you children seem to have found. I wear my oldest clothes, just as my friend Professor Anderson does, for we have been going through briar bushes, into caves and mud holes and our clothes are a sad sight. But we are not tramps."

"Is there someone with you?" asked

Grandpa Martin, looking over the man's head toward the bushes, out of which he had come.

"There was another. Anderson is his name. But he has gone to the village, and I was on my way to row across the lake to join him when I happened to pass by your tent, saw the blue light, and heard what your children said. Do you really know where there is a big blue rock like this little one that is on fire?" he asked as he pointed to the flaming blue light.

"Yes, we found a big one," said Hal.

"If you will show me where it is you will get a lot of money," said Mr. Weston. "That is, if you will sell me the meteor," he went on to Grandpa Martin. "I understand you own part of this island," he added.

"About half of it, yes. But are you looking for a meteor?"

"Yes, for a meteor, or fallen star, and the blue rock your children found is part of it. We have been looking for it a long time, my friend and myself, and we had about given up. Now we may get it. Will you sell me the fallen star?" he asked.

"I'll see about it," promised Mr. Martin with a smile. "Perhaps you will come into our tent and tell us about it. Are you—well, I was going to say the tramp—but are you the man we saw before, wandering about our camp?"

"I presume I am. I don't mind being called a tramp, for I certainly look like one. However, now that the fallen star is found I don't need to be so ragged."

"Are you the ragged man that pulled Trouble out of the spring?" asked Ted, as they watched the blue light die away.

"I did pull a little boy out of the spring," answered Mr. Weston, "though I didn't know his name was Trouble."

"That's only his pet name," laughed Grandpa Martin. "But come and sit down and tell us your story. The children have been wondering a long while what the blue light meant, and who the ragged man was. And, to-day, they've been trying to find what became of the blue rocks that Trouble made into a playhouse."

"I took those rocks, I'm sorry to say," answered the ragged man. "I'm sorry to have spoiled Trouble's playhouse. I wanted those pieces of rock, for I thought perhaps they were all I would ever be able to get of the fallen star."

"Was the blue rock really once a star?" asked Hal.

"Well, yes, a part of one, or at least part of a meteor, or shooting star, as they are called. Now I'll tell you all that happened, and I'm sorry if I have frightened you. My friend and I didn't mean to.

"Some time ago," went on Mr. Weston, "we heard about Star Island—this place that was so named because it was said a big meteor had landed here many years back. Professor Anderson and I decided to come here and see if we could find it for the museum which is connected with the college in which Anderson teaches.

"For we knew that, though most meteors are burned up as they shoot through the air before they strike the earth, yet some come down in big chunks, and we wanted such a one if we could get it. So we hunted for it all over this island. We saw you, but you were never very near. Sometimes we stayed in the cave at night, but usually went back to the mainland. All the while we were hunting for the blue rocks, for that is the color of this particular meteor.

"A few nights before you folks came here to camp, when we were digging in the ground hoping to find what we wanted, our shovel must have struck a piece of the meteor, for there was a flash of blue fire that burned for quite a while."

"We saw it," cried Ted, "and we didn't know what it was!"

"Teddy and me—we saw it!" added Jan.

"Well, that was all of the meteor we could find for some time," went on Mr. Weston. "And as that burned up—was consumed— we didn't have any. Then, the other night through the bushes we happened to come upon some blue stones, and I took them away.

"Then my friend and I hunted again to find the big piece of the fallen star, but we could not come across it. I was about to give up, but now we are all right. I am so glad! Can you take me to the big blue rock?"

"We will to-morrow," answered Hal. "It's too dark to find it now."

"You had better stay in our camp until morning," was Grandpa Martin's kindly invitation, and Mr. Weston did so.

"This meteor is a good bit like a sulphur match," said Mr. Weston. "When anything hard, like iron or steel, strikes it, blue fire starts and burns up the rock. The big piece will be very valuable.

"But we'll have to be careful not to set it ablaze. We picked up a lot of different rocks on the island, hoping some of them might be pieces of the meteor. But none was. Once I saw your little girl picking flowers, as I was gathering rocks. I guess she thought I was a tramp. Did I scare you?" he asked Janet.

"A little," she answered with a smile.

"Sometimes we stayed in a cave we found on the island," went on Mr. Weston. "I thought once the meteor might be there, but it was not."

The next day Ted, Janet and Hal, followed by all the others in camp, even down to Trouble, whose mother carried him, went to the place where the big blue rock was buried in the side of the hill. As soon as he had looked at it Mr. Weston said it was the very meteor for which he and Professor Anderson had been looking so long. They seemed to have missed coming to the hill.

The museum directors bought the fallen star from Grandpa Martin, on whose part of the island it had fallen many years before, and so the owner of Cherry Farm had as much money as before the flood spoiled so many of his crops.

Thus the story of the fallen star, after which the island was named, was true, you see, though it had happened so many years ago that most folk had forgotten about it.

A few days after Mr. Weston had been led to the queer blue rock, he and Professor Anderson, no longer dressed like tramps, brought some men to the island and the big rock was carefully dug out with wooden shovels, as the wood was soft and could not strike sparks and make blue fire.

"For a time," said Mr. Weston to Grandpa Martin, after the meteor had been taken to the mainland in a big boat, "I thought you were a scientist."

"Me—a scientist!" laughed the children's grandfather.

"Yes. I thought maybe you had heard about the fallen star and had come here and were trying to find it, too."

"No, I haven't any use for fallen stars," said Mr. Martin. "I had heard the story about one being on this island, but I never quite believed it. I just came here to give the children a good time camping."

"Well, I think they had it—every one of

them," laughed Mr. Weston, as he looked at the brown Curlytops, who were tanned like Indians.

"Oh, we've had the loveliest time in the world!" cried Jan, as she held her grandfather's hand. "We're going to stay here a long while yet. Aren't we, Grandpa?"

"Well, I'm afraid not much longer," said Grandpa Martin. "The days are getting shorter and the nights longer. It will soon be too cold to live in a tent on Star Island."

"Oh, Grandpa!" And Jan looked sad.

"But we want to have fun!" cried Ted.

"Oh, I guess you'll have fun," said his mother. "You always do every winter."

And the children did. In the next volume of this series, to be called "The Curlytops Snowed In; or, Grand Fun with Skates and Sleds," you may read about the good times they had when they went back home.

"Come on, Jan, we'll have a last ride with Nicknack!" called Ted to his sister about a week after the meteor had been dug up. In a few days the Curlytops were to leave their camp on Star Island. Hal Chester had gone back to his home, promising to visit his friends again some day.

"I'm coming!" cried Jan.

"Me, too!" added Trouble. "I wants a wide!"

Into the goat cart they piled and off started Nicknack, waggling his funny, stubby tail, for he enjoyed the children as much as they did him.

"Hurray!" yelled Ted. "Isn't this fun?" and he cracked the whip in the air.

"Hurray!" yelled Jan and Trouble.

"Baa-a-a-a!" bleated Nicknack. That was his way of cheering.

And so we will leave the Curlytops and say good-bye.

THE END

THE CURLYTOPS SERIES

By HOWARD R. GARIS

12mo. Cloth. Illustrated. Jacket in full colors
Price per volume, 50 cents. Postage 10 cents additional.

1. **THE CURLYTOPS AT CHERRY FARM**
   or Vacation Days in the Country
   A tale of happy vacation days on a farm.
2. **THE CURLYTOPS ON STAR ISLAND**
   or Camping Out with Grandpa
   The Curlytops camp on Star Island.
3. **THE CURLYTOPS SNOWED IN**
   or Grand Fun with Skates and Sleds
   The Curlytops on lakes and hills.
4. **THE CURLYTOPS AT UNCLE FRANK'S RANCH**
   or Little Folks on Ponyback
   Out West on their uncle's ranch they have a wonderful time.
5. **THE CURLYTOPS AT SILVER LAKE**
   or On the Water with Uncle Ben
   The Curlytops camp out on the shores of a beautiful lake.
6. **THE CURLYTOPS AND THEIR PETS**
   or Uncle Toby's Strange Collection
   An old uncle leaves them to care for his collection of pets.
7. **THE CURLYTOPS AND THEIR PLAYMATES**
   or Jolly Times Through the Holidays
   They have great times with their uncle's collection of animals.
8. **THE CURLYTOPS IN THE WOODS**
   or Fun at the Lumber Camp
   Exciting times in the forest for Curlytops.
9. **THE CURLYTOPS AT SUNSET BEACH**
   or What Was Found in the Sand
   The Curlytops have a fine time at the seashore.
10. **THE CURLYTOPS TOURING AROUND**
    or The Missing Photograph Albums
    The Curlytops get in some moving pictures.
11. **THE CURLYTOPS IN A SUMMER CAMP**
    or Animal Joe's Menagerie
    There is great excitement as some mischievous monkeys break out of Animal Joe's Menagerie.
12. **THE CURLYTOPS GROWING UP**
    or Winter Sports and Summer Pleasures
    Little Trouble is a host in himself and his larger brother and sister are never still a minute, but go from one little adventure to another in a way to charm all youthful readers.

Send for Our Free Illustrated Catalogue.

CUPPLES & LEON COMPANY, Publishers   New York

THE RUTH FIELDING SERIES
By ALICE B. EMERSON

12mo. Illustrated. Jacket in full colors.

*Price 50 cents per volume.
Postage 10 cents additional.*

Ruth Fielding was an orphan and came to live with her miserly uncle. Her adventures and travels make stories that will hold the interest of every reader.

Ruth Fielding is a character that will live in juvenile fiction.

1. RUTH FIELDING OF THE RED MILL
2. RUTH FIELDING AT BRIARWOOD HALL
3. RUTH FIELDING AT SNOW CAMP
4. RUTH FIELDING AT LIGHTHOUSE POINT
5. RUTH FIELDING AT SILVER RANCH
6. RUTH FIELDING ON CLIFF ISLAND
7. RUTH FIELDING AT SUNRISE FARM
8. RUTH FIELDING AND THE GYPSIES
9. RUTH FIELDING IN MOVING PICTURES
10. RUTH FIELDING DOWN IN DIXIE
11. RUTH FIELDING AT COLLEGE
12. RUTH FIELDING IN THE SADDLE
13. RUTH FIELDING IN THE RED CROSS
14. RUTH FIELDING AT THE WAR FRONT
15. RUTH FIELDING HOMEWARD BOUND
16. RUTH FIELDING DOWN EAST
17. RUTH FIELDING IN THE GREAT NORTHWEST
18. RUTH FIELDING ON THE ST. LAWRENCE
19. RUTH FIELDING TREASURE HUNTING
20. RUTH FIELDING IN THE FAR NORTH
21. RUTH FIELDING AT GOLDEN PASS
22. RUTH FIELDING IN ALASKA
23. RUTH FIELDING AND HER GREAT SCENARIO
24. RUTH FIELDING AT CAMERON HALL
25. RUTH FIELDING CLEARING HER NAME

CUPPLES & LEON COMPANY, Publishers   New York